Making It Over The Tobin Bridge

Charity C Collier

Making It Over The Tobin Bridge

This book is based on real events, people, and places.
While the names of people have been changed for privacy. The names of
places, if still open, have not.
I encourage you to visit Shannon Tavern in South Boston, MA, and
Supino's Italian Restaurant in Danvers, MA.

ISBN: 979-8-9992581-4-4

First Printing, 2025
Trask Street Press is an imprint of publisher Charity C. Collier Author,
LLC

Thank you to Leigh Nolan and Jean Allen for changing the
trajectory of my life.
Dedicated to the real Jamie Walsh.
Thank you for being a special time in my life and for the
inspiration.

I could not have published this book without giving credit to;
Development Editor: Tayler Simon of Liberation is Lit.
Editor: Marla Daniels of NY Book Editors
Book cover Designer: Justin Gerwe of Greene Street Designs

October 2024

I pride myself on living life without regrets. Sure, I've made mistakes, but I always believed that I've learned from them. This time, however, feels different. A ghost from my past, one that I'm sure will linger, is about to expose all of my carefully constructed self-assurance.

The memory came on a crisp fall morning in October 2024. Sitting there on an ordinary Wednesday, scrolling through social media, I received a LinkedIn notification for a connection request. But the name took a moment to register, so I sat staring at the picture. There he was, looking as handsome as ever, a man from my past, smiling back at me.

A wave of emotions washed over me. His words were a blur, lost in the tide of nostalgia. His message read, "Hi Charly, I hope you don't mind me calling you that. I see you are using your full name, Charleen, now, but in my mind, you are Charly. You came up as a person I may know. Seeing your name and face brought me a big smile." I let out a shaky, hollow laugh that echoed in the quiet office. *They always come back*, I'd told myself, a mantra of self-preservation. But this time, the return wasn't a victory. It was a cruel reminder of a decision I had never doubted. But it was a decision that, in this unexpected moment, was a source of profound and enduring regret.

Meeting

Spring 1994

My college journey started at the University of South Carolina–Aiken in the fall of 1991. School in South Carolina was filled with sun-soaked days, late-night study sessions—more like late-night parties—and friendships that felt like they would last forever. But, as they say, all good things must come to an end. After two fun-filled years, my grades took a nosedive, and my parents, ever the champions of practicality, insisted that I return home to Massachusetts. I was devastated but secretly relieved to return home. I had loved being away, but I'd missed my friends back home. I'd missed belonging. Despite having made great friends, I had felt like an outsider in South Carolina. Returning home, I attended the fall semester at North Shore Community College. When I left South Carolina, I was unsure where to go next. I knew I wanted to major in exercise physiology, but I wasn't sure which college program to apply to. Over the summer, I looked into two options: UMass Boston or UMass Lowell. Lowell, a town about forty-five minutes away from Danvers, where I grew up and am currently living at my parents' house, or Boston, twenty-five minutes south of Danvers, and obviously way more fun. So, I needed to attend community college while I waited to be accepted and get my credits transferred from South Carolina. It was a temporary fix, a pit stop on my path to my ultimate destination: UMass Boston. With a heart full of hope and a declared major in exercise physiology, I was ready to experience the daily grind of Boston life.

I'm from a somewhat small suburb. Growing up, it was drilled into me that education was non-negotiable. College wasn't a maybe; it was 'when you go' - no other option. My mom, an intellectual, is always reading to learn as much as she can about everything. She is an adjunct professor of history at Salem State College, and I believe that is why she has always preached education and independence to me. My dad, an engineer, graduated from the original and now considered to be the main campus of the University of Massachusetts. But let's be honest—the real unspoken rule was to go to college, find a guy, get married, and live happily ever after. Not from my parents, but the societal norm that was definitely in the air. Honestly, I'm only 21 years old and I have no idea what I want my life to look like. I mean, yeah, I'd love to find someone amazing and get married someday. But I also really want to build a career and be successful, oh, and have fun. I want to have it all, but I don't feel as though I should have to decide what takes priority at my age.

The January mix of snow and rain makes for a slow drive down Route 1 from Danvers to the Wonderland T station in Revere. Wonderland, named after the former Wonderland Amusement Park, is the beginning of the Blue Line and marks the start of my journey into Boston. Driving from Danvers to Revere and taking the T, as Bostonians call the subway, will be my daily routine for the next four months as I commute to UMass Boston.

My Hyundai Excel did well for a small car on winter roads. I am proud of my little silver Excel. I got it brand new last summer when I returned from South Carolina. The defrost needed some help, though, since it took the entire twenty-five-minute drive for all of the windows to thaw out finally. The Matty in the Morning show on 108 FM breaks for the traffic report about the backup on the To-bin Bridge and traffic delays, a familiar tune for my morning commute. It serves as a reminder of why I am not driving to campus, because I would be sitting in that right now. I pull into the Wonderland station parking lot and hand $2 to the attendant. I go into school five days a week, an extra $10 expense that I had put aside from my waitressing tips each week. I find a spot and hurry across the icy parking lot. Sliding my monthly pass through the turnstile, I pan the platform, walking to the first train car. Settling into a seat, the train is quiet with only a handful of people, and, thank goodness, it's warm.

I bury myself in my latest read, John Grisham's "The Firm," which I can't put down. After a few stops, more and more people get on, seats fill up, and people have to stand holding onto the bar overhead and swaying with the train.

"Next stop, State Street," the conductor announces, pulling me back to reality.

I gather my things and merge into the exiting crowd, looking up at the signs. I still haven't figured out the best way to switch from the Orange Line to take the Red Line to JFK/UMASS. Today, I decide to get out and switch at the State Street stop. Walking down the tunnel to the outbound Forest Hills platform, I hear a train approaching from the other side of the wall. If I miss this one, I could be stuck waiting another 15 minutes for the next Orange Line train, making me late for class. I make a mad dash, my heart pounding as I sprint down the long tunnel to the platform. I barely catch my breath as the train doors slide shut behind me.

I enjoy this routine. There is something about commuting in and out of the city that makes me feel independent and experienced. Also, I love people watching, and commuting on public transportation is the best place for that. I notice that with the same routine, I begin to see the same faces. Business people in their suits, briefcases, and work bags, heading to some office job. They always get off at Downtown Crossing. Then there are the industry workers, restaurant or hotel workers, who can be identified by their black Reebok sneakers and black pants. There may be a white button-down shirt or a branded work shirt thrown in the mix with black pants. Then there are the students. Boston is a college city, and you can tell who the college students are. They have their backpacks on, and noses in a textbook. I try to break that stigma with my black fake leather briefcase-meets-shoulder bag that I bought at Express.

After about a month, I realize that the same guy is on the State Street platform, heading toward Forest Hills, every Monday, Wednesday, and Friday. I notice him taking the Red Line and the shuttle bus to campus just as I am. He must also be a student at UMASS. I lose him once we get off the bus and head to my classes. He is incredibly handsome, at least 6'3" if not taller, with blonde hair, green eyes, and a hint of rose color on his cheeks.

Most mornings, he is already on the platform before I arrive. I wonder where he comes from, why I don't see him on my commute home. I wonder if he notices me? I frequently walk by him on purpose, hoping he will notice me. He's always standing there with his Jansport backpack, blonde hair peeking out from under a Red Sox baseball hat, exuding a confidence that makes me think he's one of the "cool" kids. I was never a cool kid in high school. I was a basketball cheerleader, which was about as cool as I got. I was able to sit with the popular girls, but I think it was because they were girls I went to elementary school with and were cool with. This guy was not my typical type. I'm not normally attracted to blondes, but something about him draws me in. I typically date men with dark hair, dark eyes, and most likely they're Italian. My now-friend, Tony, well, we haven't talked in about a year. He has green eyes, black hair, olive skin, and is Italian. When we first met in high school, I had the biggest crush on him. The feelings were not returned, but we grew to be friends. He is exactly my type.

Today, as I walk past the guy on the platform, our eyes meet and we exchange smiles, a silent acknowledgment of our shared routine. I want to initiate a conversation, but I am too scared. My mind races with all the reasons why I shouldn't bother talking to him: I am not confident enough to speak to him, I don't have anything interesting to say, and he is not going to find me attractive (although I have been told I am pretty). I know I need more confidence to talk to him, well, to speak to any guy, honestly. I need to be sure a guy is even interested in me before I am able to approach him. My past experiences haven't exactly given me much hope. I hear my mother's voice ring out in my head: *if a guy likes you, he will talk to you; guys are hunters.* He sees me. He knows I am going to the same place and never speaks to me. I'm just going to stand here and watch this cute, mysterious guy on the platform day in and day out, and most likely never speak to him. This unspoken connection continues throughout the spring semester—we never say one word to each other, not even a hello.

I've always felt a little different. Growing up biracial in an overwhelmingly white town, I never quite fit in. My mixed heritage made me stand out, not necessarily in a good way. My not black, not white, dark complexion confuses people. People ask me all the time what my nationality is, as though they cannot pinpoint what box to put me in. People would tell me I was pretty, but it felt like they were just being nice. Compared to both the girls I grew up with and famous women, I knew I wasn't the standard definition of beauty. In this suburban bubble, I know my features are unique. I have this caramel skin tone, these big, brown eyes, and a mane of brown curly hair that refuses to behave. I'm not skinny, but I'm not fat either. I work out constantly, and practically obsess over my diet. My body is the type that I can watch someone eat a salad while I drink water, and I will gain five pounds.

I always felt like I was searching for validation. It was as if I needed some guy to want to be with me, and that would prove to me that I was pretty. But the truth is, I think I am average. Guys don't exactly flock to me like they do to my friends. I've had boyfriends, sure, but usually only after they get to know me. Most of the time, I get told by guys that they like me as a friend. Maybe now that I am in school in Boston, things will be different. Maybe there will be more open-minded people who will appreciate my differences.

Summer 1994

Every summer, the popular Boston radio station Kiss 108 holds its annual Kiss concert where famous music artists perform. This year, Salt-N-Pepa, among my other favorites, will be there. My close friend Kristy and I are so excited to get tickets. Kristy arrived from Florida in ninth grade, and we have been close friends since our sophomore year of high school. She is a ball of energy and has this infectious enthusiasm. We met in the band room after school; I played the flute in the high school band during my freshman and sophomore years. I am not sure why Kristy was hanging out in the band room, but I started talking with her, and the next thing I knew, we were navigating the awkwardness of adolescence together, hanging out at the mall, going to underage nightclubs, and cruising Revere Beach to meet boys. She and I were similar in height and size, so we were able to share clothes. We still laugh because in our senior pictures, she is wearing my shirt and I am wearing hers.

The Kiss concert is held at Great Woods in Mansfield, MA, south of Boston, about an hour's drive from Danvers. Tailgating before and during the concert is all part of the day's fun, even for those who don't get tickets. Kristy and I walk around the parking lot, looking for people we might know. We run into some guys we know from Kelly's Roast Beef on Revere Beach. One of the guys, Asher, is among them. Although he doesn't know it, I have a big crush on Asher. Whenever I visit Kelly's, I check to see if he is working a window. If he is, I order my usual grilled cheese and French fries from his window to talk to him. Asher is strikingly handsome, with jet-black hair, a lean face, dark brown eyes set above high cheekbones, and a warm, welcoming smile that crinkles the corners of his eyes. He is charming, engaging in conversation, and seems genuinely interested in learning more about me. Whenever he sees me, he asks me how I am doing, what I have been up to, and where we are going, and he seems to be about my age. Sadly, he has never asked me out. This is the first time I've seen him outside of Kelly's. He is taller than I expected and has an incredible, muscular body. Kristy and I hang out with the group of Kelly's guys for a while. A few of them decide they want to go to the concert venue, so we go in with them. As we walk across the parking lot to the entry gates, Kristy leans into me and says, "How come I've never noticed how hot and jacked Asher is?"

I reply, "Um, I had no idea either. He is so hot!" *Maybe this will be a night when Asher and I can get to know each other better,* I think to myself.

Once inside the venue, Kristy and I find our seats. We'd splurged on seats under the overhang this year, unlike the lawn seats we usually got in the past. We watch several sets from different artists including Color Me Badd, Luther Vandros, and Meatloaf. When Kenny G comes on Kristy turns to me and says, "Want to go get something to eat?"

"Yeah, let's go," I reply, getting up. While waiting in line at the concession stand, we run into some guys we know from clubbing at The Palace Nightclub in Saugus. They invite us to hang out with them at their spot on the lawn. We get drinks and food and make our way through the crowd toward the lawn. Amidst the sea of flannel shirts and Doc Martens, I spot a familiar face walking toward me. He must have spotted me as well because his eyes light up when they connect with mine. What is usually the silent distance between us is gone, replaced by the electric energy of the crowd and a few too many beers.

"Hi! Wow, crazy seeing you here," he says, stopping before me, a smile spreading across his face.

"Oh my god! You're the boy from the T I see every day who never talks to me. How come you never talk to me?" I reply, my cheeks flushed, hoping I don't come off as tipsy.

"You didn't seem like you wanted me to talk to you," he responds.

"I wanted to talk to you, but I thought you may think I was a dork," I admit, shrugging my shoulder, looking back up at him in the eyes.

The awkwardness that once existed between us on the State Street platform dissolves. I feel connected, as if we have known each other for a long time.

"Ha, I thought the same thing. I'm Jamie," he says, holding out his hand, then realizing my hands are full with a drink and food.

"I'm Charly," I reply, giving him my nickname since I don't love the full family name of Charlene.

"I assume you go to UMass since I see you going to campus. What is your major?" Jamie asks. I guess he *had* noticed me.

"Exercise Physiology. I start the core of my major classes in the fall. I've been taking some required classes that didn't transfer from my previous college."

Jamie's face lights up. "That's my major! I start the core classes in the fall as well."

"Maybe we'll be in some together," I say, suddenly feeling butterflies in my stomach. I am so excited to see and talk to Jamie, and I feel silly that we haven't spoken all these months.

"I hope so," Jamie says as he smiles.

"I've got to go catch up with my friends," I say. I'd noticed Kristy and the guys had walked ahead but had stopped to wait for me a couple of minutes ago. "I'll be sure to speak to you when I see you on the T. I get on at Wonderland," I tell him, walking backward, not wanting to end the conversation.

"I take the Blue Line, I get on at Beachmont. I'll look for you," Jamie yells back.

I take one last look at him, smile, and then return to my friends. I feel intoxicated by what just happened. I cannot believe we ran into each other and finally spoke. Catching up with Kristy and the guys, she gives me a weird look.

"Who was that?" she asks.

"A guy I know from school, and I hope to get to know him better," I tell her, thinking about how I can't wait to go back to school to see him again. I should have given him my phone number.

Fall 1994

The fall semester at UMass Boston had officially begun, and a wave of excitement tinged with a hint of nervousness washed over me. Riding on the T into school and walking across campus, my eyes scanned for a familiar face. The campus, a sprawling complex of brick buildings connected by a network of overhead walkways, was a bit like a maze. I navigated the labyrinthine pathways, my heart pounding with a mixture of anticipation and apprehension.

And then I saw him when I walked into my first class. Sitting at a desk near the front of the classroom, he looked effortlessly cool in jeans, a white t-shirt with a flannel shirt unbuttoned over it, and a baseball cap. I confess I've always had a weakness for guys in baseball hats. I caught his gaze, and he smiled a slow, appreciative smile that sent a jolt of energy through me.

"Hi, fancy meeting you here," I teased. "Is this desk open?" I pointed at the desk beside him, trying to sound casual but feeling a flutter of nerves in my stomach.

"Hey, it's good to see you. Sit, the desk is all yours. What classes are you taking this semester?" he asked, his eyes crinkling at the corners as he smiled.

I showed him my schedule, a mixture of nervousness and apprehension swirling within me. He looked it over, a slow grin spreading across his face. "We're in every class together," he said, his voice a low rumble.

"No way! That is awesome," I said, facing the front of the room as the professor began to speak. My gaze kept drifting back to Jamie, and a sense of anticipation settled over me. *I hope I get to know this guy better,* I thought, taking in another glance of Jamie. *This is going to be a fun semester.*

Jamie and I quickly become inseparable. On my morning rides on the T, I sat hoping he would get in the same car as me. I rapidly scanned for him as the T would pull into the Beachmont platform. Our daily lunches at what became our favorite campus cafeteria became a ritual. Over trays of questionable cafeteria food, we shared stories of our lives. I spoke about growing up in Danvers with my parents and brother. Jamie, an only child, spoke of his life in Revere, a vibrant coastal city closer to the urban heart of Boston. We shared about going away to college, me to South Carolina, him to the University of Nevada, Las Vegas. We talked about coming home, discouraged but also missing the ways of being a person from Massachusetts. He spoke of his passion for baseball, his childhood dreams fueled by the legendary (and infamous) Little League coach, Charles Stewart, whose name would forever be etched in the city's history. I can still vividly remember getting ready for school in my junior year. I had Kiss 108 on, Matty and Billy, the cohosts of Matty in the Morning, started talking about a husband and wife who were carjacked, and the wife, who was pregnant, was shot; both the mom and the baby died. The events triggered a manhunt in the city of Boston. A week or so later, there was breaking news that it was actually the husband, Charles Stewart, who shot and killed his wife and unborn child. He had made up the whole carjacking. Then, within days, Charles jumped off the Tobin Bridge, killing himself. The Tobin Bridge is the largest in Boston, spanning two miles over the Mystic River, connecting the North Shore towns to the city of Boston.

"You're joking," I exclaimed, my eyes wide with disbelief. "*The Charles Stewart?*"

He nodded, a serious expression on his face. "I was shocked when I heard the story and heard it was him. I knew the guy; I looked up to him when I was a kid." He got quiet, put his burger down, leaned back in his chair, lifted his baseball hat, and brushes his hair back. He looked sad, and I wanted to get up and hug him. I wanted to let him know I was someone he could express these feelings with. Emotions for him ignited within me. It was more than just an attraction; it was a connection, a shared understanding of the complexities of life and the unexpected twists of fate.

Another day, while driving to Wonderland, I heard a song on the radio, and I could not believe the lyrics. I had been captivated by the beat and rhythm of the song. But when I honed in on the lyrics, I was shocked, the singer was saying he was going to have sex like an animal. This could not be allowed on the radio!

"Hey, I heard this song on the radio while coming in, the singer says it is going to fuck like an animal. It is by Nine Inch Nails. Have you heard of it? I ask Jamie.

"I don't think so, " he laughingly says. I don't think he believes me.

" I swear, I was shocked at the words, I mean, obviously they bleep out the F word, but you can tell that is what is being said. It has a good beat, which caught my attention."

"I hope to hear it and know what has gotten you so....excited? " He humors me.

One of the Exercise Physiology major requirements is to take Anatomy and Physiology I & II. This semester, we are taking A&P I. The lecture portion, held in a large, dimly lit auditorium, was one thing, but the lab... well, the lab was another world entirely. The laboratory is dark, with low-hanging fluorescent lights and full of tables and stools. Microscopes lined the cabinet counters on the perimeters of the room. I'd asked Jamie when the course had started to be my lab partner, and he'd accepted happily.

Our first task was to dissect a cat. The sight of the cats still shrouded in their formaldehyde bath sent a wave of nausea washing over me. A sleek black creature eerily resembled my beloved Raisin, my cat who had been my constant companion for eighteen years. The memory of her passing, the ache of that loss, washed over me. Tears welled up in my eyes, and I had to step out of the lab, gasping for fresh air.

"I need to get out of here," I gasped, looking at Jamie as he covered his nose and mouth with his shirt. "Please don't get the black one."

"You okay?" Jamie asked, his voice laced with concern, as I stepped back into the lab.

"Yeah, just... it reminded me of my cat," I explained, wiping away a tear. "The smell, it's overwhelming."

He nodded understandingly. "It's okay. I'll handle it. I got us a tabby cat."

I watched him navigate skinning the cat with a surprising level of dexterity. I couldn't help but notice how protective he seemed. He was calm, efficient, and considerate, ensuring I felt safe and comfortable. It was a small gesture, but it spoke volumes. Once the cat was skinned, each class we would be dissecting different parts.

"Thank you so much for skinning the cat. Now that the fur is gone, I don't feel as connected to them," I admit to Jamie.

"No, problem, I am glad you feel better. Now I can sit back for the rest of the semester and you can dissect everything," he teases me.

"I don't think so," I sarcastically respond.

That day, amidst the fumes and the unsettling sight of dissected specimens, a new understanding began to blossom between us. I was learning about him and seeing a glimpse into the kind of partner he might be— caring, considerate, and willing to take care of me.

A week later, Kristy and I sprawled on my bedroom floor while a music video blared from my television. We were deep in conversation, recapping our week, plans for the upcoming week, and catching up on all of the gossip of the people we know. Kristy picked up my dissecting kit, her brow furrowed in confusion.

"What is this?" she asked, peering at the strange assortment of tools.

"That is my dissection kit. I have to dissect a cat in my A&P lab."

"Gross, there are hairs on this scalpel. And blood on things." Kristy looks disgusted.

"Yeah, I need to wash it better next time I'm in the lab," I said, reaching for my phone as it rang.

"Hello? Hi!" I tried not to sound too excited, even though I was happy to hear the familiar voice. "Not much, you?" Kristy looked at me with a question in her eyes. I mouthed Jamie.

"Charly, you talking to the guy you don't stop talking about?" Kristy says loud enough so Jamie can hear. I swat my hands at her, mouthing stop.

"Who is that?," Jamie asks.

"My friend Kristy is over hanging out. Let me go. I will see you tomorrow." I hang up, looking at Kristy as she looks at me.

"Oh, you really like him," Kristy teases me.

"I do, but he just thinks of me as a friend," I said, a tinge of disappointment coloring my voice.

"Why do you think that?"

"Because he has not asked me out," I admit.

"Why don't you tell him you like him?," Kristy encourages.

"I can't do that!," I blurt, falling to the floor in surrender. "He's so cute. I don't have the guts to tell him I like him."

As I returned to the anatomy and physiology lab after fall break, my eyes immediately scanned the room for Jamie. There he was, sitting at our usual table, a hint of a smile gracing his lips as he saw me. My heart gave a little flutter.

"I missed you," he said, his voice a low rumble, and his hands gently rested on my knees. A jolt, like static electricity, surged through me. My mind raced, desperately searching for hidden meanings in his words, his touch. I yearned for him to ask me out, to acknowledge the simmering attraction I felt for him, and that I hoped he felt for me. I did not have the guts or confidence to tell him how I felt.

"You did? I missed you too," I replied, searching his face to find any evidence of what may come next.

"Okay, everyone, I hope you enjoyed your break," the professor said to bring the class to his attention.

The semester continues, our days punctuated by our shared lunches. We fall into an easy rhythm, navigating the cafeteria lines, finding a quiet corner to dissect our classes, and share anecdotes from our weekends. Our relationship is peculiar, teetering on the brink of something deeper. We exchange stolen glances and share intimate moments, yet the words I desperately wish to hear never seem to come. My feelings for Jamie grow with each passing day, a quiet bloom in the hidden corners of my heart. I yearn for him to say something, make the first move. I want to hear him say it, that there is a connection between us that needs to be explored. But the words remain unspoken from both of us.

As we are eating lunch in the cafeteria one day, I blurt out before I could stop myself, "Maybe we could meet up at a bar sometime," my voice a little too eager. "My friends and I go out a lot in Salem." I was hoping he would suggest that he and I hang out instead.

"Yeah, I could get a buddy and do that," he replies, his smile easy, his tone casual. My heart sank slightly.

"Why did you get two orders of fries?" I ask, noticing the extra portion on his tray today.

"Because you eat all my fries," he says with a mischievous smile. "I figured I'd get two orders so I can have a whole order."

"Oh my god, I'm so sorry! I didn't even realize I was doing that." I laugh, feeling a blush creep up my neck.

"It's okay," he chuckles, "I don't mind. I like that you're that comfortable with me. I think it's cute."

His words were a balm to my wounded pride, but a nagging doubt lingered. Was I destined to be just a friend, a comfortable companion, while he remained oblivious to the flutter of my heart every time he smiled at me?

"Are you ready for the quiz in Ms. Arnold's class this afternoon?" Jamie glances at me.

"What quiz?" Heat rises in me, I don't know about a quiz, and my anxiety causes my heart to race. "I don't know about a quiz."

"She said at the end of class on Tuesday, we were having a quiz today." Jamie confirms.

"I did not hear her say that. What's it on? I didn't study for it." I grab my notebook, looking over my notes, scanning my sloppy handwriting. I look up at Jamie, his smile looking like a Cheshire cat.

"What?" I say a little too loudly and look around to see if others heard me.

"I am joking with you." He lets out a laugh.

"What? Are you serious? Is there a quiz or not?" I plead.

"There is no quiz, I am joking with you, that is what you get for eating all my fries." Jamie sits back in his chair laughing, taking off his baseball hat and brushing his hair back, then placing his hat back on.

"You're an asshole." I exhale a sigh of relief.

"And you are a French fry-eating bandit," he teases. We both break out laughing.

"A French fry bandit?"

"Yeah, that is all I could come up with so quickly. That was pretty bad." He laughs.

"So bad."

"Come on, French fry bandit, let's get to class. We have a quiz." Jamie starts gathering his things, standing, and picking up his tray.

"Jamie, you said you were joking. Is there a quiz?" I grab my bag and try.

"No, there is no quiz, bandit." Jamie smiles, letting me walk in front of him.

Jamie took me up on the offer of meeting me out at bars. Soon, Jamie and I, often accompanied by our respective "wingmen," would descend upon the North Shore bars weekly. Within weeks, our weekend nights took on a new rhythm. The outings crackled with playful energy, a mix of friendly banter, shared laughter, and the undeniable pull of unspoken attraction. Each encounter, each shared joke, and each lingering glance fueled with what felt to me a simmering sexual tension between us.

The music vibrates through the floor at Bleachers, a chaotic symphony of '80s rock. Midnight was looming, the witching hour for North Shore bars. There was an exception to last call, the magical loophole in Lynn. The bars were allowed to make a last call at 1:30

am. Everyone knew the drill: a frantic dash to a Lynn bar to steal one more precious hour of the night.

"Hey! Shawmut for last call?" I shout, leaning close to Jamie, the music a roaring wave between us. Bleachers, with its live band, was always the loudest.

Jamie nods, his eyes meeting mine. "Okay, I'll see if I can make it."

A tiny pang of disappointment flickers through me. Still, I smile, the possibility is enough for now. He came with his friend, and maybe his friend doesn't or can't go. I give him a quick hug, the warmth of him lingering.

"Okay," I say, trying to keep my voice light. "If I don't see you at the Shawmut, Monday, then." I take the last sip of my drink, place the empty glass on the table, and turn toward the crowded exit, a hopeful flutter in my chest.

The Shawmut is a kaleidoscope of bodies moving to the beat, a mix of current hits and throwback '80s songs. Kristy and I haven't been here long when the crowd parts slightly, and I see him. My breath hitches. Jamie is scanning the room and, when his eyes find mine, a smile blooms on his face, chasing away any lingering doubt. He says something to his friend, who heads toward the bar and then Jamie is walking toward me, his gaze never leaving mine.

"Found you," he says, his voice a little breathless, a little amused.

"You made it," I reply, a silly grin spreading across my face.

"Is that okay with you?" he teases, his eyes sparkling.

"Yeah, why wouldn't it be? I asked you to come," I remind him, my heart doing a little skip. "I need to run to the bathroom, I'll be right back, promise," I say. "Would you hold my drink? Then you know I'll come back."

"Sounds good," he says, taking the glass.

As I come out of the bathroom in the small hall, standing next to a fake tall plant is Jamie, waiting for me. He hands me my drink, and I look up to thank him. But instead of words, his hand finds my waist, pulling me gently closer. He leans down, and then his lips are on mine. Everything else fades away. The music seems to soften, the voices around us disappear. It's Jamie and me, a world of just us. The kiss is electric, every nerve ending suddenly alive. When we finally break apart, breathless, I don't know what to say.

"I've been wanting to do that for so long," Jamie says, his voice a low murmur.

"I've wanted you to do that for so long," I confess, leaning back in for another kiss. His arms wrap around me, holding me close, and it feels like coming home.

"You know you drive me crazy with those short skirts," he whispers in my ear as we pull apart again, a playful glint in his eyes. A thrill shoots through me.

"Oh yeah?" I tease, a smile playing on my lips.

"The next time you wear this one, I'm taking it off you," he says, his voice husky. I gasp, a little shocked, a little excited.

"I'll remember that," I whisper back. He kisses me again, and the world narrows down to just this moment, just him.

Suddenly, the lights flicker on, jarring us back to reality. Someone yells, "Time to go! You don't have to go home, but you can't stay here!" I giggle, pulling back from the kiss, the lingering warmth of his lips still on mine. I reach up and hug him tight, not wanting to let go of the incredible feeling of being in his arms.

I spot Kristy by the door chatting with Jamie's friend. "I'll walk you to your car," Jamie offers, his hand finding mine as we head for the exit.

Sitting in my car, the feeling of Jamie's touch lingers. His lips on mine, his hand on my waist. My mind is a whirlwind of excitement and new feelings. I really, really hope this is the beginning of something more than just friends.

The following weekend stretched out before me like a blank canvas, a promise of freedom and adventure. My parents were away, off on some exotic adventure, leaving me with the house to myself. This was a familiar rhythm to my life: freedom, the quiet, the sense of boundless possibilities. When I was in high school, my parents traveled. I stayed home, punctuated by the presence of my aunt, a watchful guardian assigned to keep me out of trouble. Now, at twenty-two, I was my own guardian, my parents took my brother, and I was left alone to take care of the house.

Tonight, the adventure promised to be particularly exciting. I was hoping for a repeat of last week with Jamie. Things had been the same as usual between us the past week at school. Almost as if we'd never kissed. My winggirl this week is Marie, my best friend since third grade, when I moved across town and started a new elementary school. We'd stayed in touch through thick and thin, our friendship weathering the storms of me going off to college in South Carolina while she stayed in Danvers, enrolled in nursing school. Standing side by side, Marie is the complete opposite of me. She is petite, maybe 5'2" next to me, a tall girl of 5 8". She has dirty blonde hair and hazel eyes. I still remember the day we met; it was the first day of third grade. I was new to the school and didn't know anyone. Sitting at my desk, scared and nervous, this tiny girl walked up to me with big energy, telling me she liked my strawberry shortcake sweatshirt. She started asking me questions about who I was and what school I had been to before, and that made me feel seen. We realized we took the same bus and lived near each other. We started playing after school, and we've been best friends since. We watched her mother go through breast cancer, and ultimately pass away from it when we were in eighth grade. Marie's mom was the first person I knew to die.

I don't think I fully comprehended what had happened to my friend at the time. My parents stepped in with understanding for me, always making sure Marie was included and comfortable in our family. Marie changed after that; the once confident girl became insecure. It baffles me, because she is exactly what society considers the all-American girl, but she could not see it.

As I pull up to her house, anticipation buzzed through me. Tonight, anything was possible. I honk long and hard. Her father opens the front door. I wave, rolling down my window. "Hi, Mr. Comeau". He waves as she skirts by him towards me.

"Hi!" I say as I watch her slide into the passenger seat.

"You look nice." I lean over and hug her. She is wearing jean overalls with a white thermal long-sleeved shirt, and black and white Chuck Taylors.

"Thanks," she smiles as she settles in.

"I invited Jamie, my crush from school, to join us with a friend. I hope he shows up," I confess to her.

"Cool, that sounds fun!" she replies. As we make our ten minute drive to Salem, Marie fiddles with the radio for good music.

"Do you have any new CDs?" she asks, glancing around my back seat for a CD case.

"No, I didn't bring any with me. This cassette has some good old-school songs," I say as I press play.

"I Want to Sex You Up" by Color Me Badd starts playing. "See," I say, laughing as Marie joins me, singing along with the song.

"What is up with this Jamie guy? How come you haven't talked about him before?" She inquires.

"Ugh, he is sooo hot, we are in every class together. We spend all day together at school. I really like him. But I don't know what he thinks about me." I confess. Jamie and I spend so much time in our own bubble at school. I don't talk about him to my friends because I don't know what to say, other than I have a crush on him.

Pulling into the parking lot behind the sub shop across from the Piccadilly Philly, I find a parking spot. I check my face and apply a little more lipstick. Once out of my car, I decide to leave my jacket. Although my skirt is Cher Horowitz-short, I'm wearing socks up to my knees and a sweater—I'll be fine walking across the parking lot.

"Are you ready to get silly at the Philly?" I ask Marie as we hand our IDs to the doorman.

Once inside, we make our way to the bar. "I'll have a Bud Light," I tell the bartender, turning to let Marie tell him what she wants. My eyes scan the crowded room, then lock on Jamie. He's making his way toward me, a confident grin playing on his lips. I move away from the bar, letting Marie take my place.

"You look amazing in that skirt," he says, leaning down to give me a quick hug. The scent of his cologne is a mix of something musky and a hit of vanilla.

"Thank you," I breathe, feeling a blush creep up my neck.

"$2.50 for the Bud Light," the bartender announces, his voice gruff. I hand him a five-dollar bill, eager to escape the scrutiny of the bar and lose myself in the conversation with Jamie.

We find a spot along the wall, the bass of the music vibrating through the floor. Stone Temple Pilots' "Interstate Love Song" blares from the speakers, their raw energy perfectly capturing the mood. "They're becoming one of my favorites," I confess to Jamie.

He introduces me to his friend Brian and the night unfolds in a haze of music, laughter, and shared stories. As the clock ticks toward last call, I suggest, "My parents are away for the weekend if you guys want to come over." The words tumble out before I can entirely censor them. Jamie and Brian exchange a look, a mischievous one in their eyes.

"Sure, why not?" Jamie says, and suddenly, the night takes on a whole new, exciting dimension.

The music pulses through the house at my parents, a vibrant soundtrack to the electric energy between us. Jamie, ever the mystery man, had a case of beer in his car. We all hang in the living room, buzzing with conversation and laughter. I excuse myself to the kitchen, a playful sense of anticipation bubbling within me. Jamie follows close behind, his eyes sparkling with a mischievous gleam. As I turn, he's there, his gaze intense. He leans down, his breath warm on my face, and kisses me. The world melts away, leaving only the sensation of his lips on mine, his arms encircling me, pulling me close.

"Do you want to go to my bedroom?" I ask, raising my eyebrows and smiling.

"Yes," he says, nodding. I take his hand and lead him upstairs, leaving our friends in the living room. Once inside my room, Jamie embraces me, his lips meet mine, his hands roam my body.

"You are driving me crazy in that skirt, I told you the next time you wore it, I was going to take it off you," he murmurs, pulling back to admire me, his eyes lingering on my legs. A playful smile touches my lips.

"I remember," I reply. I slip a CD into the player, the deep beats of "Closer" by Nine Inch Nails fills the room. The lyrics echoed through the air.

Jamie chuckles, a deep, appreciative sound. "You really like this song," he observes. I grin, a mischievous glint mirroring his own.

"You have no idea," I whisper, already reaching for the buttons of my shirt. "Take off your shirt," I say. Jamie takes off his shirt as I unclasp my bra. I press my bare body to his. I kiss his chest. He runs his hands through my hair and pulls my head back. I look into his eyes, then push him toward the bed to lie on his back. I pull off his pants and climb on top, straddling him. His hands are on my breasts as I lean down to kiss him. Then I run my tongue down his chest to his belly button. I sit up and grab his hands to cup my breasts again. He sits up and begins to suck, biting my nipples.

I whisper, "I love that."

"Hey, Jamie, I gotta get going," Brian yells outside my room. I fall on top of Jamie, protecting myself from being seen if Brian walks into the room.

"Okay, man, I will be right there," Jamie yells back before wincing and saying to me, "Sorry."

"It's okay," I say as I look around for our shirts. "Another time."

Jamie grabs me and then kisses me. "We *will* do this again soon."

Jamie and Brian leave, and I drive Marie home. Lying in bed, I replay the events of the night, the feel of his hands on my skin, the warmth of his breath against mine. It's more than just sex between us, isn't it? There was a tenderness to his touch tonight, a playful intensity in his eyes that hinted at something deeper.

But were we just friends with benefits? I want to know if he feels the same way and if these stolen moments mean anything more to him than they do to me.

The silence of the night amplifies my anxieties. What if I am reading too much into it? What if I am the only one harboring these feelings? The thought of spending the next few days wondering, agonizing over every subtle gesture, every fleeting touch, is almost unbearable.

When I approach Jamie on the platform on Monday, I smile at him. He wraps one arm around my shoulder, pulling me into him and giving me a side hug.

"Hi," I say, stepping out of the embrace.

"Hi," he says with a smile as he looks into my eyes.

He doesn't seem eager to discuss what happened over the weekend, and a wave of disappointment washes over me. I try to shrug it off, to convince myself that it meant nothing more than a casual hookup between friends.

That afternoon, as we ride the T home, a strange ache settles in my chest. Today was our last day of exams, so we are officially on winter break. The thought of a whole month without seeing him feels like a cruel punishment.

"I hope we hang out over break," I admit timidly. Why am I always so nervous about expressing what I want to him?

"Of course, I want to hang out," Jamie confesses.

"It will be so weird not seeing you every day," I say.

"I know. I am so used to being around you," he says, his eyes soft with affection as he looks at me. His look makes my stomach flip.

"Next stop, Beachmont," the conductor announces. Jamie begins gathering his bag and stands up, holding onto the bar.

"Alright, I will talk to you later," he says, looking down at me.

"Yeah, call me, and we can arrange to meet in Salem," I say.

"Sounds good."

"Bye," I say, watching him walk across the platform, a familiar ache settling in my chest.

Spring 1995

The spring semester unfolds like a slow-motion dream. Jamie and I are inseparable on campus. Our days are a seamless blend of shared classes, lunches, and long, lingering conversations under the warm spring sun. The concrete campus, usually a stark and impersonal environment, transforms into our own private oasis. We find patches of grass amidst the sea of buildings to relax between classes.

Today was particularly warm, so we decided to make the most of it during our break between classes. The sun is a warm blanket against our skin. I lie down on my back, using my book bag as a pillow, watching him next to me, his blonde hair catching the sunlight. A yearning washes over me. I want him to touch me, brush a strand of hair from my face, hold my hand, any form of touch to confirm he feels for me what I feel for him.

"Have you started studying for midterms yet?" Jamie asks me.

"Ugh, no, I am dreading them," I grudgingly reply.

"Yeah, me too. What do you think you're going to do when you graduate?" Jamie questions. I still had two years until I graduated. Jamie is a year older than me, but he has more credits than me and will be graduating before I do.

"I want to work with people like me who struggle with depression, weight, and self-confidence. I want others to find exercise to help them feel good about themselves, as I did. I just don't know where that will be," I say.

"I cannot imagine you having self-confidence issues, Charly. You are beautiful and one of the most confident women I have met. You just own it. You know you are beautiful, but don't flaunt it. I think it is admirable that you want to help others."

"That is so nice to hear," I say, surprised. "I wish I felt that way about myself. Thank you."

Jamie smiles and gently rubs my leg, his hand sliding up to my hip, grabbing and shaking me. A wave of heat, a mixture of pleasure and apprehension, washes over me. His touch, so casual, sends a jolt of electricity through me. Despite the intimacy we've shared, a strange distance persists between us. It's as if we're circling each other, afraid to embrace our connection's depth fully.

"You have a big bug crawling up your jeans." Jamie pulls his hand back from my hip. I let out a scream as I sit up to brush it off.

"Where is it?" I look around, on my leg, the ground, then at Jamie, who is laughing.

"I was joking, but by how fast you jumped, you would've gotten it, or your scream would've chased it away."

"Ha Ha, very funny, you scared me. I can't stand bugs," I admit.

"I can see that." Jamie is still laughing at me as he stands. "Come on, time to get up and head to class," Jamie says, extending a hand to help me up off the ground. A smile tugs at my lips. I love how he teases me one minute and then takes charge the next. He is good about ensuring we're always on time and prepared. It's a trait we share, this innate sense of responsibility. Perhaps it comes from being an only child. Although I am not one anymore, for the first thirteen years of my life, I was. I usually am the responsible one among my friends; it is nice to have someone other than myself be that way. It feels like I am being taken care of and thought of.

As we walk back into the building, I ask, "What about you? What do you want to do?"

"I think I will start as a personal trainer, but my ultimate goal is to work in sports training. I want to train athletes," Jamie says, his expression full of ambition. He holds the door for me, his hand resting lightly on the small of my back as he guides me through. Another jolt courses through me. I turn to him, my heart pounding a rapid beat against my ribs.

"You will be great at that. I hope I will be able to get some personal training sessions from you," I tease, winking at him.

"Oh, you will," He says with a wink back. I steal glances at him as we walk side-by-side to class, his easy stride, the way the sunlight catches the gold in his hair. I desperately want him to reach for my hand, to acknowledge the connection that exists between us.

A familiar face breaks my reverie. It's a girl I recognize from one of my classes last spring semester, and we had gotten to know each other. She and I exchange niceties quickly. Her eyes, however, linger on Jamie, that unmistakable spark of interest flickering in her gaze. I have noticed a lot of girls on campus looking at him like that, it seems others are as drawn to him as I am. She glances at me, a curious expression on her face as if trying to decipher the dynamic between us. Oblivious to the attention he commands, Jamie smiles and greets her politely.

"How do you know her?" Jamie asks as we continue to class. I hope he doesn't press for information about her. If he expresses interest in her, I will be crushed.

"Oh, I know Meredith from my first semester here," I respond as casually as possible.

"She is definitely a South Shore girl," Jamie says.

"What does that mean?" I ask him.

"I can tell the difference between a South Shore girl and a North Shore girl," he explains.

"Could you tell I was from the North Shore when you first noticed me?" I inquire.

"Charly, I'm surprised you made it over the Tobin Bridge," he replies. I can't help but laugh as I think about how much of a North Shore girl I am and how proud I am of it. I love where I grew up and wouldn't change it for the world. The North Shore are the towns that line the forty miles of the coastline north of Boston. The South Shore are the towns from Boston south to Cape Cod.

"What is a South Shore girl like?" I ask him.

"They didn't have as big of hair in the 80's, and they tend to be more crunchy granola compared to North Shore girls." Jamie explains.

"Oh, I never saw it that way, but now that you say it, I can see that."

Jamie wraps his arm around my shoulder and pulls me into a side hug. He loves to give me these side hugs. He then kisses the top of my head.

"You should have seen my big hair when I was in high school," I share with him.

"Oh, I've seen the pictures. I've been in your bedroom, remember?" He laughs and winks at me as I step out of his embrace. I love the way he teases me. He is exactly what I want in a man, and I wish he felt the same way about me. Yet, as the weeks pass, I, who usually wear my heart on my sleeve, find myself strangely guarded with him. Fear creeps in, whispering doubts in my ear. Am I reading too much into his playful banter, his lingering touches?

One night, a few weeks later, fueled by the energy of the night, the lines blur. After the bars closed, I find myself driving to Revere, to his apartment, my heart pounding a frantic rhythm against my ribs. As I pull up to the triple-decker he lives in, a wave of nervous excitement washes over me. He is waiting for me outside, a hesitant smile gracing his lips. He walks around my car, opens the passenger door, and gets in.

"My mom is away for the night, so you can stay over, but we have to get up early because she will be back first thing in the morning," he whispers. "I will help you find a parking spot."

It's an impulsive decision, born from desire and a fleeting moment of vulnerability, and hopes of a night filled with passion. I do have some fear that this will change everything, that he will only see me as a hookup. But I don't stop myself. Once in his bedroom, he tilts his head down and our lips meet. He embraces me around my waist as he pulls me closer. I wrap my arms around his shoulders, pulling myself as close to his body as possible. I feel his erection against my stomach, arousing me even more. He pulls my shirt up over my head as he bends down to kiss my breasts. I reach around, unlatching my bra to release them. His hands cup me, his fingers playing with my nipples. I grab the hair from the back of his head and kiss him hard, my tongue in his mouth, my lips absorbed in his.

"I want to feel you inside of me so bad," I whisper as I pull back slightly.

He moves me closer as we remove the rest of our clothes and get on the bed and he moves up my body on top of me, kissing my thighs. He slides the top of his finger inside of me. I suck in a breath and groan. He feels so good. He pulls himself up and sucks on my breast, keeping one hand in between my legs.

"You feel and taste so good." He looks down at me, his gaze connecting with mine. He reaches to the bedside and unwraps a condom. At the same time, I reach down and stroke his erection. He leans over and kisses me as he slides inside. My back arches and my hands wrap around his torso. Our bodies begin moving in a primal dance, a passionate interplay of desire and urgency. Each thrust is electric, sending waves of pleasure coursing through me, igniting every nerve ending.

Gently running his hands up and down my legs he says, "Your legs drive me crazy."

He rolls me over, pulls up my hips, and slides inside me from behind. He's so deep inside me. He thrusts, hard.

"That feels so good. I love that. Don't stop," I beg. His thrusts increase as he pulls my hips into him, in rhythm with his thrusts. I lean my face into the mattress and scream. "Fuck, you are going to make me explode." I say to him, "I am, Jamie, I am." He begins to get faster and harder.

"I am going too....uh, fuck, Charly." Jamie roars. I feel his body stiffen, then soften as he lies over me, cupping my breast.

"Wow," I say as we collapse into the mattress.

I lay next to him, my heart pounding, wanting to surrender to the feeling that this was more than just a fleeting encounter. I can still feel his hands on my hips, his lips on mine. The way he cupped my breast. The way he felt inside me. I want this all the time. I start to hear his deep breaths of sleep. I roll over and look at him from the streetlight glow outside his window. I could do this every night. I want to do this every night. I can't fall asleep between wanting to remember every moment of being here with him and fearing that his mother will come walking into the apartment at any moment.

Sometime later, daylight begins to fill the room. Jamie starts to stir. I want to stay like this forever, but this is not how I want to meet his mom. He pulls me closer to him and spoons me. "Morning," he says, kissing my shoulder.

"Morning," I say and snuggle closer to him. I feel his erection against my body.

"We have to get up, but I want you one more time. Let's be quick," he says as he lifts my top leg, bends my torso forward, and slides inside. Relaxing into him, I feel safe and protected with Jamie. I have not felt like this before with a guy - I want a life with him.

Summer 1995

It is quiet as I walk into my parents' house. Once again, they're away for the weekend. And I can't stop thinking about Jamie when I am not with him. It has been a whole school year of us being inseparable at school. I still cannot figure out how he feels about me. I am confused by the whole situation.

I'm sitting here alone in my bedroom after being out with friends, when all I want is to talk and be with Jamie. *If he were my boyfriend, he would be with me right now,* I think to myself. Looking at the time, 12:30 am, *is Jamie home and awake?* I pick up the phone and call. I hope I don't wake his mother.

"Hello?" he answers quickly but sounding sleepy.

"Did I wake you?" I whisper, not even saying who I am.

"No, I was lying on the couch watching TV," he says, knowing it's me.

"Do you want to come over? My parents are away," I tell him, hoping he will say yes. "I get scared being here alone, and I would really like it if you were here with me."

"Yeah, I'll head over soon."

"Okay, I'll see you then." As I lay on my bed, I have about 30 minutes until he gets here. It gives me time to think about how I am going to tell him that I have feelings for him. That I would like to see if we can take whatever this is we are doing into a more dating situation. Maybe even boyfriend and girlfriend. I really don't like having to initiate "the talk". I wish he would just say, "Charly, be my girlfriend." But that is not happening, and I don't want to keep guessing; it is time I know what is going on.

Opening my eyes to the sun filling my room, I realize it's morning. Feeling slight pains in my head and dry mouth, I think, "*Ugh, hangover. Crap, I have to go to work.*" Wondering what time it is, I look at my clock to see it's 9:50 am. My lunch shift starts at 11. I remember calling Jamie to come over, but he didn't show up because I didn't hear the doorbell. Needing to get ready for work, I quickly shower and dress in my uniform for Supino's, the restaurant where I waitress. I don't have time to call Jamie now. If it's slow, I'll call him from work. Running down the stairs from my bedroom, I grab my keys and head out.

Charly & Jamie 1995

As I step out the door, the sun blazes and the heat is already oppressive. My eyes drop to the porch stairs. "Am I forgetting anything? Keys, apron, check folder. I have everything I need." I slip behind the wheel, driving the familiar route to Supino's. Once there, the aroma of garlic and basil always hangs heavy in the air as I navigate the maze of tables. Supino's, with its regular patrons and staff who have been working here forever, is a cornerstone of the North Shore, a haven for families and friends. It originated as a takeout place across the street in a shopping plaza, but I am unsure when they moved into this building to become a full-service restaurant. When I was young, it was only takeout, and my father would bring me along to pick up lunch or dinner. I would stand next to him, looking around at a tapestry of vibrant reds and yellows. There were oversized clowns seemingly watching our every move. The clowns were a thing. When I started waitressing, I asked the owner about them, and he said his mother loved clowns, so she decorated the place with them.

Today, the lunch rush had been a blur, each minute an agonizing eternity away from the moment I could finally speak to Jamie. Now, back in the sanctuary of my room, the answering machine blinked ominously. A wave of apprehension washes over me as I hit play.

'Hi, it's Jamie. Call me when you get home.'

My fingers tremble as I dial his number, the anticipation fluttering in my chest. His warm baritone voice answers, sending a jolt through me.

"Hello?"

"Hi, it's Charly. What happened last night?"

"Hey there," he chuckles, "I was about to ask you the same thing. I came by, but you never answered the door."

"I fell asleep. I'm so sorry."

"I was really looking forward to seeing you."

"Me too. But the good news is my parents are still gone. Would you like to come over tonight? I promise to stay awake."

He laughs a deep, resonant sound that makes my heart skip a beat. "I don't think so, you blew your chance last night." Hearing his words felt like a gut punch; I could feel my throat tighten and a lump in it.

"Oh," I manage to get out.

"I'm joking, Charly, I'd love to." He laughs, "Seriously, I am joking, I can be there around nine?"

"Not funny." I take a deep breath. "I mean, if you don't want to, you don't have to."

"Charly, I want to come over. I was giving you a hard time," he assures me.

"Okay, nine is good. I'll be here wide awake! I'll see you later."

"See you later, bye, Charly."

I gaze at my watch. It is 6:30 p.m. My eyes sweep across the room. I need to clean my room and change my sheets. I will have dinner, shower, and relax on the couch until he arrives. I decide to get take-out, a roast beef, the staple sandwich of the North Shore. I have been eating the razor-thin slices of roast beef on a hamburger bun since

I was a little girl. Back then, I would get it with cheese and mayo; now, I do the junior size "three way" cheese, mayo, and a secret almost BBQ-style sauce. I love that my parents' house is one street from downtown Danvers, and I can walk to most of the places I like to go—the mall, the library, or any shop downtown. Although walking from Danvers High School felt like a never-ending journey when I was heading home in high school.

Walking into the roast beef sandwich shop, I see Elaina working. She gives me a big smile.

"Hi, Charly! How are you?"

I notice Gio's head pops up from behind the roast beef slicer. Gio is a staple at the shop. He is always back there building our sandwiches. Everyone knows him and he makes sure to say hello to everyone.

"Hi, how are you?" he asks in his Greek accent.

"Hi, Gio," I wave back. Looking at Elaina, I say, "I'm good! How are you? How is school going?" Elaina, who attends Endicott College in Beverly Farms, Massachusetts, replies, "It's going great! What can I get you?"

"Can I get a junior with mayo, cheese, and a small fry?"

"That will be $4.25."

Handing her the money, I glance around and see the Peggy Lawton ChocoChip cookies on the rack at the counter. "Oh, can I get these as well?"

"That will be $5.00 total."

She hands me the bag of food.

"Have a good night, thank you!" I say, grabbing the food and turning to leave, when in walks my two friends, Jen N. and Michelle. The three of us have been close since tenth grade, when Jen N. had to transfer to public school after attending a private Catholic school previously.

Michelle Andrews and I became friends in seventh grade. She entered my life like a burst of sunshine. She sat next to me one day at lunch and talked to me as if she had known me her whole life. Pretty sure her first words to me were, "Ryan is super cute right, want to come over and watch Pretty Woman this weekend? My sister got the tape." Unsure, why was she talking about Ryan to me, but talking about boys and watching a movie, what more does a girl want at that age? Our friendship blossomed effortlessly, a bond forged in shared laughter and antics. She is still a ball of energy, with her jet-black hair, fair skin, and freckled face.

"Hey, guys! What's going on?" I happily ask them.

"More like, where have you been? We tried calling you to see if you wanted to hang out with us," Michelle demands.

"I was working all day. I'm just grabbing some dinner now. I can't hang out tonight, a friend from school is coming over."

"Who?" Michelle asks, surprise lacing her tone. She isn't used to not knowing every person in my life.

"A guy named Jamie," I reply with a smile.

"Ooohh, is he just a friend?" Jen N. chimes in.

"Not really, there is something more," I admit.

"Have fun having lots of sex," Michelle says.

"I will!" I exclaim as I walk out.

Jen N. and my friendship, unlike with Michelle, didn't start off well. When my parents moved us into the house on Trask Street in third grade, even though I had never met Jen N., and she didn't go to my elementary school, for some reason, she didn't like me. She would make fun of me all the time. It was torture every time I had to walk by her house to get to another friend's house.

But it all changed in junior high. I began to fit in with a group of girls who went to Smith Elementary. They lived in the prep area, known for its split-level houses surrounding St. John's Preparatory

High School, an all-boys school. Jen N.'s father lived in that neighborhood. Because of that, she was friends with one of the girls I became friends with, Brittany Whitehead. Brittany had a sleepover with all of us, and that is when Jen N. and I ended up becoming friends. After that day, we would hang out at each other's houses after school, go to the mall together, and become good friends. I loved having a friend just a few houses away from mine.

Sitting at the kitchen table, I devour my roast beef and fries, every bite fueling the anticipation building within me of Jamie coming over. A quick shower washes away the lingering garlic and fried scents left over from my shift at Supino's. I slip into a t-shirt and boxers, feeling a surge of excitement. The couch beckons, and I cozy up under a blanket, happy to find out there is a Lifetime movie on. A guilty pleasure, I know. I tear open Peggy Lawton's Choco Chip cookies package, which always reminds me of when I was a little girl getting take-out with my dad. The clock ticks away, each minute an eternity, as I wait for 9:00 PM for Jamie to arrive.

A loud knock at the door startles me awake. Blinking, feeling disoriented, I glance at the living room clock at 9:05 PM. Thank goodness I'd fallen asleep downstairs! Peeking through the living room window that looks onto the porch, I see him, tall and handsome, standing there at the door. I rush to the mirror and quickly check to ensure I don't look like a zombie. To my surprise, I look... good. Maybe even a little sexy. A mischievous grin plays on my lips.

My breath hitches as I swing open the door. He looks incredible. His blue eyes widen in surprise, a hint of a smile gracing his lips. At that moment, I realize that I am doing the right thing by telling him how I truly feel.

"Hi," I said, a shy smile gracing my lips.

"Hey you," he replies, his voice a low rumble sending shivers down my spine. He steps closer, the air between us suddenly thick with anticipation. I reach for him, intending a hug, but he tilts his head and captures my lips, catching me completely off guard. His arms encircle me, a warm, familiar embrace. I melt against him, the world fading away. The hard muscles beneath his shirt send a tingle through me.

"Let me lock up," I murmur in his shoulder, "and then we can go upstairs. Do you want something to drink? I have Brisk Iced Tea or Coke."

"Can I have a glass of water?" His voice is husky.

"Sure," I say, hurrying to the kitchen, my breath rapid from nerves.

I watch from the doorway as he explores the living room, his gaze lingering on the framed photos of me and my family. He turns, his eyes meeting mine, and his eyes sparkle as he approaches me. I hand him the water, my fingers trembling slightly. My stomach does a nervous flip-flop. He is so incredibly handsome. It's hard to believe he is actually here with me. I know I'm not unattractive, but compared to him... well, I feel like a sparrow beside an eagle. He takes a sip of water, his eyes looking directly into mine. I take a sip of my iced tea, trying to appear nonchalant, but my hands are still shaking.

"Come on, let's go upstairs to my bedroom," I finally manage, my voice a little breathless.

In my room, Jamie looks around, his eyes taking in every detail, making me realize how little I'd truly let him see before. He sets his glass down on a side table then turns toward me, his eyes darkening. The scent of his cologne, a heady mix of Calvin Klein Obsession and something clean and fresh, fills the air between us. He runs his fingers through my hair, my stomach does another somersault, and my legs feel weak beneath me.

"Did you do anything tonight?" he asks, his voice a low growl.

"No," I admit, avoiding his gaze. "I just stayed home, watching TV, waiting for you." I try to sound playful, but there's nervousness in my voice.

He gazes at me, his eyes holding mine captive. He lifts my chin, his thumb gently stroking my lower lip. Then, his lips touch mine, a slow, tender kiss that sends sparks flying. He kisses my ear, my neck. I moan softly, lost in the sensation. I pull back, eager, my eyes wide with a mixture of fear and exhilaration.

"Jamie," I whisper, "I... I like you. More than just a friend. I want to be more than friends."

He smiles, a slow, breathtaking smile that lights up his entire face. "I'd like that very much. Charly, will you be my girlfriend?"

The blood rushes to my face. I nod, a breathless laugh escaping my lips. "I thought you'd never ask."

He pulls my head closer and kisses me. I'm kissing my boyfriend, Jamie Walsh.

"Let's go lie down," I suggest, motioning toward the bed.

A giddy warmth spreads through me as I lay beside him, our bodies intertwined. I can't believe this incredible man is officially my boyfriend, here, in my bed, with me. He traces a lazy path with his fingers down my side, and every nerve in my body feels ignited. His arm tightens around my waist, pulling me closer, and I melt against him, sighing contentedly. His lips brush mine, a feather-light touch that engulfs a fire within me. I can't help but smile a smile that mirrors the happiness I feel. He gently tucks a stray curl of hair behind my ear, his eyes twinkling with amusement.

"My beautiful girlfriend," he whispers.

"My handsome boyfriend," I reply, snuggling closer to him. Rolling on top of me, he leans down to kiss me, his lips parting mine. Sitting up, he takes off his boxers and reaches for a condom. I slide my underwear off. Leaning down, sucking my breast, he slides his hand between my legs, his fingers exploring me, then entering me.

"You're so wet," he says.

"I can't wait for you to be inside me," I whisper.

As he sits back, he bends my legs, falls forward, and pushes into me. I gasp in enjoyment. I wrap my arms around him.

"Harder," I whisper. Jamie begins to thrust harder and faster.

"Yes, you feel so good," he groans.

He rolls me over and pulls my hips back toward him so I'm on my knees. He slides back into me. He grabs my hair, causing me to arch my head and back.

I moan, "Jamie, don't stop. You make me feel so amazing." He continues pushing into me, speeding his thrusts. "Does that feel good?" He asks me. I turn my head, looking him in the eyes. "It feels perfect." I pant.

"Fuck, Charly, you turn me on so bad. I am not going to last....I am going to..." His breath shortens, and he trusts harder. I let out a moan as I climax. He speeds up letting out a roar of "Yes." as his body slows down and softens. He pulls back onto his knees and slides onto the bed next to me.

"Charly, you make me feel incredible." He turns his head, looking at me.

"You do the same to me," I whisper to him.

As I lie beside him, the lingering warmth of our encounter still buzzes through my veins. The moonlight casts long shadows across the walls. I follow the lines of his face, along his strong jaw, tracing my fingers down to his chest, admiring the way his muscles ripple beneath his skin. He is simply irresistible. But it isn't just his physical beauty that captivates me; it's the way he makes me feel desired and seen. In his arms, I feel safe, protected. I snuggle closer, burying my face in his chest, inhaling the comforting scent of his skin.

"Good night," I whisper, my voice thick with contentment.

"Good night," he murmurs, his arm tightening around me, his lips pressing a soft kiss to my hair.

Charly 1995

*A*s I step out the door, the sun blazes and the heat is already oppressive. My eyes drop to the porch stairs. "Am I forgetting anything? Keys, apron, check folder. I have everything I need. I step, almost stepping on it. What is that? It's a condom stuffed with breakfast sausages. What in God's name? A wave of nausea washes over me. Bizarre. Absolutely bizarre. And scary, if I'm honest. Who would do this? Why here? I scan the street searching to see if anyone is watching me. I don't see anyone or unusual cars on the street. Relief washes over me, quickly replaced by a cold dread. I grab a paper towel and a plastic bag from the kitchen, my hands trembling slightly as I retrieve the... the object. The dumpster behind the restaurant will have to do. I climb into my car, the engine a welcome roar against the pounding of my own heart.

The drive to work is a blur. I think about the possibility of Jamie leaving that thing on my parents' steps. I can feel tears surfacing. I blink them back. I don't want to walk into work having cried. I am working with Melissa, she will be all over it. She and I have become friends from waitressing together. She is a feisty Italian girl. Because she has long, loose curls and brown eyes, from the back, people confuse us. She cares about me; combined with her feistiness, she will want to kick whoever's ass it is who has made me cry. It had to be Jamie; he was on his way to my house. I don't know why he would do something like this. But I can't think of anyone else who would do it. I mean, he does little pranks on me from time to time. But I feel this is more of him making it clear that he only sees me as a casual fling—just a friend with benefits. I am so angry and hurt. How could he leave that condom filled with sausages on my parents' front steps? Even if this was just a friends-with-benefits situation for him, leaving that condom was incredibly disrespectful.

I feel disappointed. I thought I was doing things right with Jamie. But here I was in the same position I keep finding myself in with guys. I am either just a friend or a placeholder girl. The girl a guy hangs out with until the girl he wants as his girlfriend comes along. I am not the girl that guys come over and talk to when I go out with girlfriends. I often hang back while my friends get picked up. People tell me I am attractive, so I guess it is my personality. But I don't know what part of it turns guys away. I make friends quickly. I get along with most people. I don't understand why guys only see me as a friend. I was hoping it would be different with Jamie.

For the next few weeks, I avoid Jamie's calls. I don't know what to say to him. I got his message loud and clear. I can't see how I can continue to be his friend. Once the semester starts, I have to figure out how to avoid him. I am driving to campus this semester rather than taking the T because I finish my courses at 11:30 a.m. That will keep me from running into him and traveling home with him.

When classes start, I quickly realize that Jamie and I are not in any classes together. It's funny how we went from every class together and inseparable to not seeing each other at all. I am two weeks into the semester, and I already miss him. There is a girl named Jessica who is friendly with Jamie, and they went to high school together. She can be outright rude to me, so I keep my distance. But today I run into her.

"Hi Charly, how are you?" she asks. I am a bit thrown off that she is talking to me, but I'll take the opportunity to ask about Jamie.

"I am good. How is your semester starting off?" I ask her.

"Oh, you know, trying to figure out where things are," she says.

"Yeah, it is crazy how you can have one class in the McCormack building and then have 15 minutes to go over to the other end of the science building," I say, trying to continue the conversation. She does not respond to me but keeps walking with me. "Have you seen Jamie? I haven't seen him since classes started," I say, hoping she will give me an answer.

"Nah, he's so wrapped up in his girl. Those two are all in love, as always. He is nowhere to be found," she replies.

Hearing her words is like a punch in the stomach. I feel the heat rise in my body. I take a deep breath and blink not to let the tears in my eyes flow. So, that was what was happening. Jamie had a girlfriend. Had he been with this person the whole time, or was it a new thing? I am nauseous and can barely breathe. "Oh," I say to Jessica, trying to sound like I knew he had a girlfriend. "I am heading to the parking garage. Have a great rest of your day," I manage to say without breaking into tears. I cried the whole drive home from school. Jamie and I never saw or spoke to each other again.

Charly & Jamie 1997

"Congratulations," Jamie says, raising his glass to toast me.

"I still can't believe it," I say, "I'll probably get a letter saying I need to take one more class and that I'm short on credits."

"I know the feeling. That's how I felt last year," he says, laughing.

"Maybe tomorrow, when I have the diploma, I'll feel like I've graduated. I can't imagine what life will be like without school. I've been in school for 19 years." I chuckle at that thought. I had thought that after I'd completed my last project - the dreadful group project - and presented it to everyone, I would feel as though I was done. That project came out horribly, and I am reminded that group projects are the worst. Not everyone pulls their weight on them. I hope I never have to do one again.

"It is a strange feeling," he agrees.

Jamie surprised me with dinner at the Black Cow in Hamilton. First, we stopped by my grandparents' house, even though they're coming to my graduation tomorrow. We can't be in Hamilton without visiting them. My grandmother gave us $25 toward dinner. Sitting there, enjoying the meal and the company, a feeling of profound contentment washes over me. Two years. Two incredible years with Jamie, although if we count the year we were hanging out before we decided to be boyfriend and girlfriend, it has been three years of something between us. He is my best friend, my confidante, my lover. We're building a life together, sharing dreams, supporting each other's goals, and pushing each other to be our best selves. He sees me, truly sees me, cherishes me, and makes me feel safe and adored. And oh, how I adore him. His presence still has the power to take my breath away. He is the most handsome man in any room, and the fact that he's mine still feels like a fairytale.

"So, I've been thinking," Jamie begins, his expression suddenly serious. My heart lurches. Is this... is he breaking up with me? This is how those conversations start. "At the end of the summer, we should move in together."

Relief washes over me, stronger than any fear. "Really?"

"Yes, it feels right. Three years, and we're still living with our parents, juggling schedules to grab overnights here and there. I want to wake up beside you every morning, come home to you every night. I want to start building a life with you."

"That's the sweetest thing you could ever say," I say. "Though you should know, I'm a terrible cook."

"I know, but I enjoy cooking." He grins, his eyes twinkling.

"Yes, I want to move in together. I want to make a home with you. Where do you think we should look?   I'll be working in Marblehead, and you're in Saugus."

"Maybe Revere?" he suggests, knowing there is no way I'd move to Revere.

I gave him a playful look. "Let's brainstorm."

As we drive back to Danvers, I gaze out the window at the familiar houses. I've driven this route countless times since I was a child. The homes are beautiful, many with manicured lawns and towering pine trees. In the fall, the foliage is a breathtaking spectacle. New England has its charms, despite the brutal winters.

"Mind if I just drop you off? I'm exhausted and need to get some sleep before tomorrow," Jamie says, rubbing his eyes.

"Of course. I'll drive to your place in the morning. Would you mind driving into Boston from there?" My graduation was at the Bayside Expo Center, near UMass Boston.

He pulls up to my parents' house. The lights are dim downstairs, a sure sign they are already asleep.

"Not at all. See you in the morning, college graduate." He leans over and kisses me, a lingering kiss that sends shivers down my spine.

"Good night. Drive safely. Call me when you get home, okay? I love you." I always say it, just in case something happens to one of us. I want our last words to be "I love you."

"Love you too. I will."

Jamie watches me walk into the house, a wave of happiness washing over me. I flash the porch light as a signal that I'm safely in the house. As I climb the stairs, I pause in my room, my eyes drawn to the cap and gown lying on the bed. It feels surreal, like a costume for a role I'm about to play—the role of a young woman embarking on a new chapter filled with love and promise.

Graduation day is a whirlwind of excitement. Mo Vaughn, a Red Sox legend, receives an honorary doctorate, Donna Summer belts out a powerful rendition of the national anthem, and even Cookie Roberts graces us with her presence to deliver a keynote speech. Though we Exercise Physiology majors are a small contingent, we make our voices heard. My classmates and I, in a moment of pure elation, led a spontaneous cheer, our voices echoing through the arena: 'AHHH, BEEP, BEEP, TOOT, TOOT!' in honor of the legendary Ms. Summer.

Afterwards, Jamie and I drive back to Danvers, eager to celebrate with my family—Jenna, Marie, and the rest of our loved ones. We feast at Supino's, the warmth of family and friendship surrounding me. As I look around the table, a wave of pure joy washes over me. Years of hard work, late nights, and countless cups of coffee have finally culminated in this moment. Holding that diploma in my hands, a tangible symbol of my accomplishment, feels incredible. This is a victory I earned, a milestone I could never lose.

Charly 1997

The last week of classes before graduation is a total disaster! I am battling a nasty cold, probably from overdoing it. I am juggling school, my job,

The last week of classes before graduation is a total disaster! I am battling a nasty cold, probably from overdoing it. I am juggling school, my job, an internship, and a little bit of partying. I have a huge group project due, and I feel like I am barely hanging on. This project is the last thing standing between me and graduation, and we have to present it in class. I drag myself to school, and my professor, thank goodness, can totally tell I am a walking, zombie-looking mess. He lets me go home, which is an appreciated relief.

As I am leaving, Peter Finley stops me. Peter and I became good friends this semester, even though we'd had classes together before. We chatted in classes and got to know each other better, but it was nothing like what happened between Jamie and me last year. Peter is more of a fun classmate that I have gotten to know. We didn't spend time together outside of class.

To my surprise, Peter asked me to the graduation ball! I am totally shocked and say yes without even thinking. I assume it's just as friends because I've heard him mention having a girlfriend before. I ask our mutual friend about it because if he does have a girlfriend, I don't know why he would ask me. Mike tells me they broke up a couple of months ago.

Ironically, Peter is tall, blonde, and totally ripped, like Jamie. Blondes aren't usually my type, but Peter is handsome and has such a great personality. It just isn't the same spark I felt with Jamie.

Peter tells me to get some rest and says he'll call me to make plans for the ball. I am excited, and I still can't believe I am graduating. I am waiting to hear from my advisor that there is a mistake, and I still have one more class to take.

A few nights later, Peter calls as he said he would. We discuss arrangements for the ball at the Fairmount Copley Hotel in Boston.

"You should totally wear your Dress Blues!" I suggest teasingly to Peter. "My mother would be thrilled if you showed up at the house in it."

"I am impressed you know what they are called," Peter says. "I will think about it." Peter had entered the Marines right out of high school and served in Desert Storm in Kuwait. He is now in the Reserves. He does one weekend a month and two weeks a year.

The night of the ball is filled with fun, laughter, and celebration. I wear a full-length red sequined dress that hugs my curves and makes me feel like Jessica Rabbit. Peter arrives at my parents' house looking handsome in a blue suit, set off by a light blue tie to bring out his eyes.

"Wow, you look so handsome," I say to Peter as he enters the house.

"You look incredible, you clean up well," Peter says, smiling at me. I laugh, smoothing my dress. I realize that Peter only sees me in gym clothes. I had become more casual in how I dressed for school, especially since I often went straight to my fitness center internship after our classes.

My mom insists that my dad take pictures of us, as if we were going to prom. Honestly, I don't mind because this is my last time attending *a function for school ever again. In a week, I will graduate with my Bachelor of Science in Exercise Physiology and complete my education.*

Gushing over us, my mom says, "You two look so good together, such a good-looking couple."

I give my mom a look of 'what are you talking about'. She knows Peter and me are just friends. As we head out, I remind my parents that I am staying out for the night. I am 25 and still telling my parents whether I am coming home or not.

The Fairmont Copley Hotel's ballroom is a Renaissance period style, featuring large chandeliers and gold and off-white decor. Built in 1912, the hotel still retains the charm of that period. Graduates and their guests enter with excitement. Conversations and laughter fill the room with the background sounds of silverware and glasses clinking. The evening unfolds with dancing, drinks, and a formal sit-down dinner, spent with friends and other classmates. There are plenty of shared laughs throughout the night, and Peter and I are playful and flirtatious the entire evening. While dancing, Peter kisses me several times, and we share make-out sessions on the dance floor. It takes me by surprise, but it also ignites something within me. While we are slowly dancing, after another kiss, Peter confesses that he has feelings for me, surprising me. Peter never appeared to have romantic feelings for me before tonight. I thought that he thought of me as only a friend. I am unsure of how I feel, as I like him and our friendship. I feel as though I can be myself around him, and he makes me laugh. Tonight I feel physical chemistry with him, so perhaps I should see where this goes.

After the exhilarating ball, Peter and I head to our classmate Tammy's apartment in the South End, a short walk from the hotel. Tammy is dating Peter's best friend, Tom, and the four of us plan to spend the night. We'd left our overnight bags in Peter's car, so we head out to retrieve them.

Lost in the maze of the hotel, we stop to ask a woman for directions to the parking garage. Dressed in a short black leather skirt and boots, she looks like she stepped out of a nightclub. "It's at the end of the street, right before the building ends," she points. "And boys, be careful of your ladies. This is a highly prostituted area." I couldn't help but smirk at Peter, my eyes widening playfully.

"Sounds exciting," I tease, looping my arm through his. He grins and gently squeezes my hand as we continue our search.

Tammy's apartment is cozy, and she offers us the extra room with a futon. "I hope you guys don't mind sharing a bed," she says with a knowing smile.

"Not at all," I reply, my heart fluttering. We had shared some unforgettable kisses at the ball, and the thought of spending the night with him, even on a futon, fills me with thrilling anticipation.

"As long as you don't mind my snoring," Peter jokes, his eyes twinkling.

"You snore?" I tease back, already picturing us curled up together, the comfortable silence punctuated by the soft rhythm of our breaths.

"I'm just kidding," he assures me.

The moment I wash off the makeup and let my hair down, I feel a flutter in my stomach. Looking at myself in the mirror, I catch a glimpse of the woman I am becoming—confident, beautiful, and ready for whatever the night holds. With a quiet thrill, I hope that Peter feels the same way.

Back in the room, the darkness is broken only by the soft glow of the streetlights. As we lie side by side, sharing whispers and laughter about the evening, a comfortable silence falls between us. Then, his hand reaches out, tracing the contours of my face, his fingers gently tugging at my hair. I lean into his touch, our lips meeting in a kiss that ignites a fire within me.

Our bodies are entwined as a symphony of touch, exploration, and sounds. His hands roam over my skin, sending shivers down my spine. I feel small and cherished in his embrace, his strength a comforting anchor. As our clothes fall away, there are no words, just the unspoken understanding of our desires.

He moves over me, his body a perfect fit, larger than I anticipated, filling me with a sensation that takes my breath away. I arch my back, my nails digging lightly into his shoulders, a low moan escaping my lips.

"You feel so good," I whisper, lost in the moment.

"You too," he murmurs back, his voice rough with passion. Our bodies speed up to a staccato rhythm. I can hear his breathing building. "I am going to .... oh god, Charly." He lets out a groan as he slowly descends in thrusts. He kisses my breast and falls to the side of me. I lay there, realizing what just happened, shit.

Morning brings with it a mixture of exhilaration and uncertainty. What did last night mean? Was it just a fleeting encounter, or was there something deeper between us? The memory of his touch, the intensity of our shared passion, lingered like a sweet ache. I had built walls around my heart after my experience with Jamie, but with Peter, it feels as though he wants me.

He stirs beside me, his eyes opening and meeting mine with a sleepy smile. He pulls me close, his lips brushing against mine in a gentle, lingering kiss.

"That's a nice way to start the day," I think, a smile gracing my lips. The uncertainty remains, but so does a glimmer of hope. Yes, perhaps this is the beginning of something truly special.

We join Tammy and Tom for breakfast, strolling through the charming streets of the South End. Peter is playful and affectionate, his hand brushing against mine as we walk. It feels like we're one of those couples you see in movies, carefree and happy, strolling through the city.

The air is warm and alive with the sounds of the city. The rumble of garbage trucks, the honking of horns, the rhythmic sweep of street cleaners. It's early summer, the air thick with the scent of coffee and freshly baked pastries. Tiny buds on the trees hint at the vibrant blooms to come, and I feel a sense of belonging, a thrill that only the city can provide. I know it is not love, but I love the way I feel with Peter—carefree, excited, and completely myself.

Later that day, as he drops me off, Peter asks when we can see each other again. We decide to celebrate the eve of graduation with a night out in Boston, catching a live band and letting loose. One last hurrah before we officially enter the "real world."

We head to the Harp, a legendary Boston bar across from the old Boston Garden. We're hoping to catch The Cattunes, my favorite cover band, but they aren't playing tonight.

Still, the night is magical. We dance, we kiss, and the air crackles with undeniable energy. It feels like hanging out with my best friend, but there's an underlying current of sexual tension that I can't ignore. I know I need to spend more time with him to understand the depth of our connection truly.

Since Peter lives in Somerville, a city just outside Boston, I had picked him up. Driving back to his parents' house, Peter suddenly commands me.

"Hey, pull into that parking lot." He points to a parking lot coming up on our right.

"Why?" I ask, as I follow his instructions.

"I want to spend more time together," he admits. "Pull over right there."

The urge to spend more time with him becomes overwhelmingly exciting to me as I park the car and look at him. He reaches across, *pulling me closer to him. We start kissing, our passion growing with every touch. Before we know it, we're lost in the moment, the city lights fading into the background. I climb on top of him, our lips still locked, as he lowers the seat back. He unbuttons his jeans as he slides them and his boxers down. I shimmy my underwear off and pull up my skirt. He reaches under my top and bra, caressing my breasts. I reach down and guide his erection inside of me. Holding onto the seat, I ride the wave of pleasure, our breaths fast and excited. I moan as I lower my head.*

"This is so amazing," I whisper.

"Charly, you feel incredible," he says.

Suddenly, the beam of headlights cuts through the darkness. I scramble to cover myself, mortified. An officer taps on the window, his voice stern. "Move along, folks," he says.

Flustered, I move into the driver's seat as fast as I can. I start the car, driving out of the parking lot as quickly as I can. We both burst into laughter, the adrenaline of the encounter still coursing through us.

My graduation is an exhilarating and profoundly satisfying experience, though a pang of sadness lingers as Peter, unfortunately, chose not to attend. However, my heart swells with joy as my parents, brother, and grandparents are there watching. My mother, in particular, is ecstatic that Donna Summer, a legendary singer from the Dorchester neighborhood, has been invited to perform the national anthem. The Bayside Expo Center, overlooking the picturesque Dorchester waterfront, serves as the magnificent backdrop for our graduation. The atmosphere is electric, charged with the excitement of graduating stu-

dents and the overflowing pride of family members witnessing their loved ones achieve this momentous milestone.

Following the ceremony, a celebratory luncheon is held in my honor at Supino's. Since I work there, it's become my family's go-to place. My extended family and dearest friends, Marie, Michelle, and Tony, join me in celebrating this incredible accomplishment.

The summer of 1997 is a whirlwind of excitement. Having transitioned from my internship, I am fully immersed in my full-time role at the Jewish Community Center's fitness center. Anticipation buzzes within me as I await an offer for the Assistant Fitness Director position, having recently interviewed for the role.

Tony and I rekindled our cherished friendship, especially after he attended my graduation lunch. Tony being there made me feel as though he was putting effort into our friendship. We became friends at Chess King in the Liberty Tree Mall when we were teenagers. I had a major crush on him, and we dated for a little bit. In my senior year of high school, he started dating a girl who did not like him and me being friends. He became distant, and we lost complete contact when I went to school in South Carolina. When I came back and heard he had broken up with her, I reached out to him. Now, as young adults, our friendship has become like brother and sister.

Tony rents a charming Beacon Hill apartment, which quickly becomes our summer sanctuary. My days off are spent basking in the city's vibrant energy and exploring its hidden gems with Tony. We stroll through the city, often grabbing a cappuccino in the North End, Boston's Little Italy, soaking in the summer sun and enjoying lively conversations. Tony is my confidante, my advisor, and a profound influence on who I am becoming. He has an air about him, a sense of European sophistication that he instills in me, a feeling enhanced by his father, who grew up in Italy, and his mother's warm Italian American heritage. Soccer is a passion deeply ingrained in Tony's life, thanks to his father's coaching and his childhood summers spent playing in Italy.

Spending time in the city also brings me closer to Peter, who works at a fitness center in Boston. My early morning schedule, from Sunday to Thursday, allows me to fully embrace the city's vibrance during late afternoons and its weekend charm. After-work drinks, leisurely lunches in the Boston Gardens, and idyllic picnics amidst the summer sun are part of our cherished routine. It is a summer of exploration, friendship, and pure joy.

The summer air crackles with the electricity of starting a new chapter in life. My relationship with Peter feels like we are stepping into adulthood. Gone are the endless phone conversations; our connection thrives on experiences we have together. One sultry July evening, we decide to ditch the outside world and indulge in a horror movie at his house. "Scream" was the chosen victim, despite my aversion to the genre, but it was Peter's sad attempt at peer pressure. It was more of the promise of a thrilling night that won me over. I pick up the VHS at Danvers Video on my way to Somerville.

Running late, I snatch a small bag of Fritos from the snack stash for my brother and me. My mom always made sure there was something good to snack on. Fritos are my favorite, providing a welcome crunch as I navigate the summer traffic, eager to reach Peter's house.

Opening the door, Peter greets me with a warm smile and a quick kiss.

"Sorry I'm late," I say, feeling a blush creep up my neck.

"No worries," he assures me, leading me down the dimly lit hallway. The wood-paneled walls are adorned with framed photos of his siblings. We pass through the formal dining room and into the living room, where his mother sits, engrossed in a book.

"Hi, Mrs. Finley," I greet her with a polite smile.

"Hi, Charly, how are you holding up in this heatwave?" she says, her voice gentle yet firm. Mrs. Finley, a former schoolteacher and now a formidable force in education administration, is a woman of few words but immense strength. I can't imagine raising seven children, let alone excelling in her career.

"Do you guys want to order some food before we start the movie? Mom, are you hungry? Are you up for some takeout?" Peter asks, his attention divided between us. His attentiveness to his family, especially his mother, is a quality that deeply impresses me.

"I'll have whatever you get," his mother says, her gaze still fixed on her book.

"I'm not starving right now. I had some Fritos on the way over," I admit, looking mischievously at Peter.

"Yeah, I know," he teases, his voice playful, "you came in kissing me, stinking of Fritos."

I laugh, slightly embarrassed, and say, "Sorry."

"Peter, be nice," Mrs. Finley says as she lowers her book, looking at Peter over the rim of her glasses.

"It's all good, Frito breath," he retorts, turning to me, his smile widening. "Still enjoyed the kiss. Chinese sound good to you?" he asks, turning to his mother.

Peter is effortlessly witty and endearingly attentive. His good looks, of course, are an added bonus. His height, piercing blue eyes, and sculpted physique, developed through countless hours in the gym, make him a vision. But it is his personality, his playful banter, and his genuine kindness that truly captivate me.

Our favorite date nights are Boston nights, unfolding like a vibrant tapestry. Nights of laughter echoing through cozy bars, the magic of live comedy filling the air. Our dates are a delightful blend of city excitement and quiet moments. Weekends occasionally find us on the picturesque Cape Cod, visiting his brothers and his beloved grandmother.

A thrilling road trip to Six Flags in Western Massachusetts further cements our bond. In turn, I introduce him to my extended family. Our friendship, a sturdy foundation, blossoms into a romantic relationship that unfolds organically.

In the peaceful embrace at his brother's Hyannis, MA, home one morning, my heart awakens. As I watch him sleep, a wave of emotions washes over me: joy, happiness, and a profound sense of contentment brim in my chest. The urge to touch him, to feel the warmth of his skin against mine, is irresistible. The thought of waking up beside him every day, of dedicating my life to his happiness, fills me with a quiet ecstasy. He is the source of my joy, the reason my heart sings.

He stirs, a slow smile gracing his lips as his arm, strong and warm, encircles my waist, holding me captive in his embrace. "Morning," he murmurs, his voice a low rumble against my ear.

"Morning," I whisper back, snuggling deeper into his warmth. He gives me a gentle kiss, a fleeting touch that ignites a spark within me. His hand, bold and exploratory, finds its way beneath my shirt, sending shivers down my spine. I respond by wrapping my leg around him, my hand seeking him out, finding him ready and eager.

"Mmmm," I moan, lost in the deepening kiss. He pulls me closer still, his body hovering over mine, his lips trailing a path of fire across my neck. With a swift, confident move, he strips away my clothes, his gaze burning into mine. Then, he's inside me, his movements strong and sure, yet gentle and tender. I arch my back, a low moan escaping my lips.

"Shh," he whispers, his eyes searching mine.

"Sorry," I mouth, remembering his family might be close by. But the urgency of our passion silences all other thoughts. We move in unison, a symphony of bodies and emotions. I surrender to him completely, lost in the intoxicating rhythm of our lovemaking. As he moves

within me, I realize I love him. I don't tell him, out of fear that he doesn't love me back.

Peter and I are enjoying a night out with his friends in Boston a few weeks later. Laughter fills the air; the city lights a vibrant backdrop to our easy camaraderie. Later, at his friends' apartment, exhaustion begins to creep in. I find myself drifting off on the couch, the murmur of their conversation a distant lullaby. Then, I hear,

"She is great, Peter," His friend says, her voice light and airy.

"Yeah, she is. I like her a lot," he replies, his tone casual, almost indifferent.

A chilling silence follows, seeming to stretch on forever. And then, the words that shatter my world: "But I miss Lisa."

The blood drains from my face. My breath hitches in my throat, the world tilting on its axis. A wave of nausea, sudden and violent, threatens to consume me. I lay there, paralyzed, listening to their voices drift away. I did not hear the rest of the conversation due to the ringing heat in my ears. Lisa, I remember her name. The woman he was involved with while we were in college. The woman I'd thought he was still with when he asked me to go to the graduation ball. He misses her.

I know, with a certainty that pierces through the fog of disbelief, that something has irrevocably changed. This wasn't just a casual remark, a fleeting thought. It was a confession, a yearning for someone else. And in that moment, I feel a profound sense of loss, a crushing disappointment that threatens to consume me.

I need to get out of here. I want to get far away from him. The apartment, once a haven of warmth and shared laughter, now feels suffocating. I walk into the kitchen, my voice trembling slightly as I tell Peter I need to go home. His confusion is palpable, but I can't explain. The words are caught in my throat, a raw and painful lump. I have to leave to escape the suffocating weight of his words, the shattering of my illusions.

Sleep eludes me when I am lying in my bed. I toss and turn, replaying Peter's words in my mind, each syllable a tiny dagger. The morning brings a wave of devastation. I need to escape this suffocating silence in my bedroom. My phone sits mockingly on the nightstand, a silent testament to my evanescent happiness. I long for it to ring, to hear his voice, but the thought of talking to him also feels unbearable.

Desperate for solace, I drive to my grandparents' house in Hamilton, MA, a 20-minute drive from my parents' house. The familiar landscape offers a fleeting sense of calm, with rolling hills and quaint horse stables. In the summer, one can hear the distant rumble of polo matches echoing through the air. Memories of childhood summers spent here, watching riders gallop past the house, flood back, offering bittersweet comfort.

My grandparents are surprised and overjoyed to see me. I break down, pouring my heart out to my grandmother, the words tumbling out in a torrent of tears. She holds me close, her gentle touch a soothing balm against the pain. We sit in the backyard. I lie back in the lounge chair, the warm sun filtering through the pine trees, a temporary reprieve from the storm raging within me. The lush green lawn stretches before me, the scent of freshly cut grass mingling with the earthy aroma of the woods beyond. A small patch of trees marks the edge of their property, a gateway to the mysterious swamp that lies half a mile into the woods.

I must have drifted off to sleep because I open my eyes to see my grandmother walking toward me.

"Charly, you fell asleep. I didn't want to disturb you," my grandmother says, her voice filled with concern. "Do you want to stay for supper? I'm making hot dogs and beans. I may have a box of mac and cheese I could make as well."

"Yes. Grandma, I would like that very much." My voice cracks as I hold back my tears. Being at my grandparents' always

brings a comforting return to childhood. I think of Peter's grand-mother, her vibrant spirit slowly fading as dementia steals her memo-ries. I remember our last visit with her at her home in Cape Cod: her bewildered gaze, her heartbreaking apology for not recognizing me. "If I have met you, I am sorry, I don't remember you," she had said, her voice filled with confusion. The memory of that encounter and the pro-found sadness her disease brought to his family adds another layer to the bond I have been forming with the family. I had fit in with his family; they had accepted me and included me in their sphere.

That night, I make the difficult decision to end things with Peter. Talking to him on the phone, I didn't mention the overheard conversa-tion, choosing instead to cite a growing incompatibility. He didn't ar-gue, a chilling acceptance hanging heavy in the air. Once I hang up, I feel numb, doubting my decision. Should I have talked to him about it? Maybe I should've told him how I felt about him more; I never told him I loved him. Did I love him? If I loved him, would I be able to end things so quickly? Ugh, I am not good at this relationship stuff. I keep messing things up. I think I just made a mistake.

Charly & Jamie 1998

"F "Five, four, three, two..." Looking around at our friends in our apartment, it's about to be 1998. Jamie and I are both working in our fields, and we live together. Our place is in an old Victorian house converted into apartments on the Peabody-Danvers line. It is a convenient location, right in the middle of our jobs. I love the tall ceilings and hardwood floors. We decorated it with light, yellow colors to brighten up the place. I never imagined my life would turn out this way. I'm so in love with Jamie, I love our life and, as far as I'm concerned, this is happiness and perfection.

"Happy New Year!" Jamie exclaims, kissing me while bending me back.

Laughing, he swoops me back up. "Happy New Year, love you," I say to him as I step back to straighten up from being dizzy.

"Charly!"

As I look at Jamie saying my name, he's getting down on one knee. *What's he doing? Is that? Yes, it is, a diamond ring!* I look around and our friends are watching us in anticipation.

"Will you marry me?" Jamie asks. I thought I was dizzy from Jamie bending me backward. But my head is spinning now. *Oh my God, oh my God.* I start shaking, I'm in shock.

"Yes, yes, of course, I will marry you!" I say, pulling him up to stand.

"Thank God!" He laughs. "I love you so much."

"I love you too." I can't believe this is happening. I can hear our friends cheering, but I can't stop kissing him. Pulling back, I laugh, "We're getting married?"

"Married."

"Married?"

"Married, jeez." We both laugh as we reference *Sixteen Candles*. I look down at the ring on my hand.

"January 1, 1998, we got engaged," I say jumping up and down, looking up at Jamie.

He pulls me close and hugs me. "Yes, we did."

"Congratulations!" I hear as we enter my parents' house. I thought we were just coming to my parents' New Year's brunch with them. I notice Jamie's mom, Sandy, and my grandma and grandpa here too. My dad is shaking Jamie's hand.

"You all knew?" I ask everyone, surprised.

"Of course! You didn't think Jamie wouldn't ask us for our blessing, did you?" my mom says, handing me a mimosa. Turning to Jamie, he gives me a wide-eyed look, smiles, and shrugs.

"I know you've always wanted to get married at Glen Magna. If you want that, we need to secure a date," my mom says as we all sit down to eat brunch.

"Glen Magna sounds perfect."

"Do I have a say in anything?" Jamie asks playfully.

"Of course, but my dream has always been to get married at Glen Magna, the estate at Endicott Park here in Danvers. I mentioned that to you before when we went to the champagne reception during the Danvers Family Festival," I explain, looking at Jamie to indicate I don't want to discuss this further right now. I want to bask in the excitement of getting engaged to him.

"Oh yeah, that is a very nice place," he agrees.

"Mom, please let Jamie and me enjoy our engagement. When we know what we want to do, we'll let you all know," I say, looking around at everyone.

My mom, Jean, is deeply embedded in the community and her social calendar is always full with friends. She and my dad, John, have a vibrant social circle, filled with dinners and parties. My relationship with my mom feels like a well-worn path, a typical mother-daughter dynamic. There's an unspoken blueprint she holds for my life —a vision I've largely adhered to. Yet, beneath the surface, there have been rifts, quiet disagreements over choices I've made that didn't quite align with her expectations. The college application process brought this into sharp focus through her disapproval of Johnson and Wales in Rhode Island. And although never fully articulated, it has always hung heavy in the air. Since my return from South Carolina, the pressure has eased, replaced by her obvious delight in my relationship with Jamie and the prospect of marriage. My life is finally aligning with the trajectory she envisioned. But a quiet truth lingers: her desires aren't always my own, and it's in those moments that the delicate balance between us can tilt.

Birthdays have always held a special place in my heart. Growing up, my mom would throw fun parties at places such as the Ground Round—who didn't love throwing peanut shells on the floor, and parties making ice cream sundaes at Putnam Pantry? As I got older, I took the reins, planning celebrations with my closest friends. Before Jamie and I got together, my girlfriends and I would go out to Boston to have dinner and dance at clubs. This year, I want to do something special with Michelle, Marie, Kristy as I plan to ask them to be my bridesmaids. Jamie and I have set our wedding date for Friday, June 4, 1999. We choose June 4th because it is the date of the Kiss 108 concert in 1994 when we first spoke after months of stealing glances at each other on the T.

Marie is still my anchor and confidante all these years, since the early days of whatever it was Jamie and I were doing. Since then, she has helped me navigate my insecurities in my relationship with Jamie, and I have helped her with her relationship with Matt through the ups and downs. We are each other's refuge, always there to lend a shoulder to lean on.

The lasagna, a testament to my limited culinary prowess, bubbles gently on the stove. My mom, a culinary magician, would have scoffed at my modest attempt, but this one actually tasted... decent. I arranged the table, placing a small card in front of each place setting.

Kristy, ever punctual, arrives first, laden with appetizers, giving us a few moments to catch up on life. Then Michelle bursts through the door, a magnificent chocolate cake in hand.

"Happy Birthday!" she says, her voice booming. Marie, predictably, is late. I love her dearly, but her tardiness could test the patience of a saint.

"Okay, ladies, find your name card, that is your seat," I announce.

Finding their cards and taking their seats, they eagerly opened the envelopes I'd placed on their plates.

"Ahh, *yes*!" Michelle squeals, her eyes wide with delight.

Marie, however, hasn't touched her card. "What is it?" she asks, her voice filled with confusion.

"Marie, open it!" I urge, a hint of impatience creeping into my voice.

She finally opens the card, and then... tears.

"Oh my God, you want me to be your maid of honor?" she cries, her voice trembling.

"Of course!" I exclaim, bewildered by her reaction. "I didn't realize you would be so emotional."

"I'm sorry," she sobs, wiping her eyes. "I have something to tell you."

My heart pounded. "What is it?"

"I'm pregnant."

The words hang in the air, a bombshell. "What?!" I exclaim, my jaw dropping. Looking at the others, they are just as shocked as I am.

"I know it's early," she says, her voice catching. "But we went to Puerto Rico... and well, I got sick. Really sick. Then I missed my period, and I went to the doctor. She thinks I conceived around Valentine's Day, which makes sense, considering Matt and I went skiing that weekend."

"Oh my God!" Kristy gasps. "When are you due?"

"End of October," Marie replies, a small smile playing on her lips.

"Way to steal my thunder," I joke, though a genuine wave of joy washes over me. "Don't worry, we're not getting married until June 4th, 1999."

"Thank goodness!" Marie laughs, wiping away the last of her tears. "I'll have time to lose the baby weight."

"Marie!" I scold gently. "You're having a baby! That's far more important than your weight."

I'm getting married, and my best friend is having a baby. It feels surreal, like we are becoming real adults. Does that mean we will have to start acting like them as well?

By September, the wedding planning is in full swing, my mother acting as both my enthusiastic cheerleader and my most formidable critic. Thankfully, the chaos is a welcome distraction from the profound shift that has occurred within me. Jamie and I have seamlessly woven our lives together, a comfortable rhythm settling over our days. Two months after I graduated, I applied for the open position as the assistant fitness director at the Jewish Community Center where I had been interning, and I got the job. I am now more involved with developing programs, classes, and motivating the members. I design monthly challenges and teach step aerobics classes. Jamie, meanwhile, embarked on a bold new chapter, leaving the familiar terrain of the fitness industry to pursue a challenging career in sales at Cyrk, a marketing company where other people I knew were getting jobs.

We had found our footing as an engaged couple, our weekends a kaleidoscope of social adventures. The summer brought us lazy weekend mornings at home together until we headed up to Gloucester to Good Harbor Beach. Sometimes we enjoy a ride up Route 1, crossing into New Hampshire to find the vibrant energy of Hampton Beach and the arcades, with the joyful chaos of flashing lights and playful competition, especially the thrill of skee ball or air hockey. But for me, it is always about the fresh-squeezed lemonade vendor on the boardwalk. A sweet nectar with a hidden treasure of sugar at the bottom. I became an expert at the art of finding that perfect sip, with a bit of sugar and lemonade.

As fall came too fast—typical for New England—there are evenings spent with my dearest friends, sharing stories over dinner or gathered in cozy apartments. And Jamie, with his childhood friends, sometimes ventures into the city for the roar of a Red Sox game or the electric energy of the Celtics. Through every adventure, every shared moment, the sweetest part of it all for me is the quiet comfort of knowing that no matter where our days took us, we would always end up home together. Although, I always seemed to get home before Jamie.

Charly 1998

On October 15th, 1998, I stand amidst the bustling chaos of Madrid-Barajas Airport, two bags in tow. Armed with the phrase "estación de tren"—train station—I navigate the throngs of travelers, searching for a taxi. The city unfolds before me in a kaleidoscope of colors and sounds. Cars whiz by, scooters weave through the traffic, and the air crackles with an energy I've never experienced before. Fear and excitement warm me as the taxi driver expertly navigates the busy streets.

Reaching the train station, I'm thrown into a flurry of activity. I look for the ticket sales windows, and announcements blare in a language I barely understand. Finding the windows, I approach the ticket counter and take a deep breath. "Un boleto de Málaga," I stammer, hoping I haven't butchered the pronunciation. The ticket agent responds in a torrent of Spanish, but I manage to decipher the meaning from his gestures and the exchange of coins.

With my ticket clutched in my hand, I embark on a thrilling scavenger hunt, deciphering track numbers and platform signs. Thank goodness for numbers being universal. The train, a sleek silver serpent, awaits. I settle into my seat, anticipation bubbling within me. The Spanish countryside unfolds like a breathtaking panorama—rolling hills, olive groves, and quaint villages whizzing past. I'm traveling to stay with Sylvia and Mario, family friends, since their son, Antonio, stayed with us during my eighth-grade year. Mario will be waiting for me in Málaga. This is more than just a visit; it's an adventure, a leap into the unknown.

I have no concrete plans, no itinerary, no set goals. I'm here to explore, to get lost in the labyrinthine streets of Spain, to soak up the culture, to learn the language, and to discover myself. I remember meeting Sasha, a British girl who lives near Paula, Sylvia and Mario's daughter. She challenged me to find her and to seek out new friendships. The thought of it sends a thrill coursing through me. This is just the beginning of my Spanish adventure.

Mario picks me up at the Málaga train station and drives me to their charming house. They are incredibly generous, even offering me a job washing dishes at their restaurant. The next day, Sylvia patiently explains the local bus system, pointing out the stop just down the street. Feeling a surge of excitement, I hop on the bus and head toward Fuengirola, a picturesque beach town nestled along the Mediterranean.

My destination is the women's clothing store where Sasha works. The shop is a vision in white, and the saleswomen are impeccably dressed in matching suits. I feel a wave of self-consciousness. As I browsed, I couldn't help but admire their confidence, easy laughter, and effortless grace.

Then I see Sasha. Standing amidst the racks of clothing, she exudes an effortless chic air that makes me feel a touch underdressed. But my insecurities fade as she smiles, her face lighting up in recognition.

"Hi, I don't know if you remember me. I'm Charly. I met you in the spring. I'm Paula's American friend," I said, my voice a little breathless.

"Of course! I see you're back," she replies, her posh British accent adding a touch of sophistication that I secretly envy.

"I've decided to move here," I announce, a thrill coursing through me.

"That's bold. Not many Americans would do that. Good for you," she says, briefly scanning the store as if to gauge the time.

"I'd love to get together sometime," I say, eager to reconnect.

"Sure, here, let me write down my number," she offers, walking toward the cash register. Scribbling her number on a piece of paper is a small act that feels like a passport to a new adventure.

"I'll call you soon. I don't want to keep you from work," I say, glancing around the store.

"Don't worry, we're closing soon anyway. Siesta time!" she says with a playful smile.

I laugh, realizing I had a lot to learn about Spanish customs.

From that moment on, Sasha becomes my unofficial guide to Spanish life. I quickly adapt to the rhythm of the day: the leisurely lunches, the two-hour siestas, and the late-night dinners. Meeting friends for coffee at a bustling plaza becomes a cherished ritual.

I also meet Nico, a charming man whom Sasha introduced me to. To my surprise, he runs a casting agency and asks me to help find people to put on his books. I immerse myself in the exciting world of film and television, assisting in casting extras for commercials and music videos. The vibrant energy of the sets and the glimpse into the behind-the-scenes magic are all exhilarating. On the days at the casting studio we are putting together pictures of people to match the casting requests of the production company. Some days, it's pure excitement as we host casting calls, with the director and production team right there, witnessing them decide who they want. And those set days? They're a wild, sixteen-hour adventure, where every moment is a piece of the story coming to life. I think the most significant thing I have learned is about lighting. I am shocked at how they can film while dark out, and on film it looks as if it is the middle of the day.

Sasha, Nico, and I become an inseparable trio, exploring the local bars and restaurants and enjoying lively conversations late into the night. I am living in Europe and wouldn't trade it for the world. Both Sasha and Nico have spent extensive time in the United States. This brings me comfort because they often understand my American ways. They have to remind me often to slow down. Life in Spain is about being present and enjoying life. Nico, being older than us, shares his wisdom around finances. Sasha, who has made her own way, often offers sound advice on how to integrate into Spanish life. I think I offer them the American optimism that you can have anything you want in life, as long as you work for it.

My days washing dishes at Mario's restaurant are filled with laughter and learning about Spanish men. I am the only woman and the only American working at the restaurant. The cooks and waiters seem to find me intriguing. They love to ask me questions about America. I have been asked many things like "do you have a big house and a big car," or "does everyone have a gun," and "why are you mad at President Clinton?" I feel like the unofficial American spokesperson. It is so interesting to learn what they think of America and Americans. As I stand behind the bar scanning the restaurant, my eyes stop on a guy. He is captivating, with dark hair, eyes like melted chocolate, and a mysteriousness. I've seen him a few times, enjoying leisurely lunches, always returning my fleeting glances with a shy look. But my halting Spanish holds me back. I have no idea who he is, but I want to know him.

On a rare night, Nico and I find ourselves without Sasha at Old Town, our favorite bar, when the mystery guy walks in with another man and a woman. My heart leaps. I cannot tell if the woman with him is accompanying him or the other guy. To my surprise, Nico says hi, clearly knowing the man, and shakes his hand.

"You know him?" I question Nico.

"Who, Colin?" Nico assumes and turns his head to where the group is standing across the bar.

"Yeah, I have seen him around town and think he is so cute. I have been scared to talk to him because my Spanish is bad. He speaks English?" I ask Nico.

"As British as they come," Nico says, chuckling. As I watch Colin from afar, I make a decision: I will not let this opportunity slip away. I wouldn't approach him tonight, but I am going to figure him out, and hopefully, he will be interested in getting to know me.

Fueled by a bottle of wine over dinner the next Saturday night, I declare to Sasha, "Tonight, we're on a mission. I'm going to talk to Colin."

"To Colin night!" Sasha exclaims, raising her glass in a celebratory toast.

We bar-hop, searching for him amidst the throngs of people. Crazy Daisy's, Eagles, and even a few dimly lit dive bars we usually avoid but nothing. Disappointment begins to set in. Then, just as I am about to give up, I see him. My heart pounds against my ribs. Sasha perches precariously on a bar stool and cheers me on mischievously. The air is thick with the scent of cigarette smoke and the intoxicating buzz of the crowd. I navigate the throng of dancers, my eyes fixed on Colin. He seems to be watching me, a slow smile playing on his lips.

Finally, I reach him. "Hi, I'm Charly," I say, leaning in to be heard over the music. My voice trembles slightly, but I press on. "I've seen you around, but I was too intimidated to talk to you. I thought you only spoke Spanish. I barely speak Spanish myself!"

"I've seen you too," he replies in a soft British accent. "I thought you were Spanish and was too nervous to talk to you. I speak Spanish, but when I am nervous, I sometimes botch it."

I smile at his British term. Relief washes over me, followed by a surge of unexpected exhilaration. "You're cute," I blurt out, completely unfiltered by my usual inhibitions.

"You're cute, too," he says, a playful glint in his eyes. "We should go out sometime."

"I'd like that," I say, my heart pounding. "Take my number." He takes out his phone and puts it in as I yell it out to him, feeling a giddy sense of accomplishment. Walking back to Sasha, I beam. "Mission accomplished!" Sasha declares, throwing her arms around me. Tonight, under the starry Spanish sky, I know I took a leap of faith, a small act of rebellion against the cautious girl I used to be. And it paid off. In my solitude in Spain, no eyes on me, I have shed the need for caution; my actions flow freely, unseen by my mother or childhood friends.

But Colin did not message me in the week that passed. On a quiet Sunday night, Sasha, Nico, and I sit outside Crazy Daisy's, enjoying drinks, when Colin walks in. I wave at him, and Colin waves and nods, and continues walking into the bar. Turning to Sasha and Nico, I grimace and say, "I guess he doesn't like me. I never heard from him, and that was a major brush-off."

Sasha gives me a sympathetic look while Nico says, "Fuck him," and walks away to get more drinks. About 20 minutes later, Colin walks up to me.

"Hiya, how are you doing? I just got back from a shoot. I was gone all week. Do you still want to get together sometime?" he asks.

"Oh, what do you do?" I reply and smile because I find his accent charming.

"I'm a focus puller for commercials and music videos," Colin says. I appear to be surrounded by people in the film production industry.

"Oh, cool," I say, even though I have no idea what a focus puller is. "Well, when I didn't hear from you. I figured you weren't interested in going out. What changed your mind?" I question him.

"Oh, I see. Well, I am interested in getting to know you. I was traveling to a work shoot. When I am working, I focus on work. The shoots are long days, sometimes lasting 14 hours. I figured I would contact you when I got back. I didn't realize there was a rush. But I do want to get to know you."

I think about his answer. I understand about the long shoots. But I think about what it would be like with someone who would not communicate with me while away at work.

"So, did I blow my chances with you?" He cocks his head a bit, examining me, as if he is trying to read the answer on my face.

"Almost, but I will give you one more chance." I squint my eyes, giving him a stern look.

"Okay, I promise I will message you tomorrow, and we can set up a time," Colin says.

"Sounds good," I reply with a smile.

"Bye then," Colin says as he walks away.

The next morning, my phone buzzes with a text message from Colin. Texting was still a novelty in the US, but it was already commonplace in Spain. I quickly learn the ropes—prepaid phones, rechargeable cards with credits to text or call, a system far more advanced than anything I was used to.

We arrange to meet up a few nights later at Old Town. The weekday nights bring a quieter energy to the bar, a welcome change from the weekend crowds. As we talk and learn about each other's lives, I find myself captivated. Colin looks as though he could be Spanish, although he is as British as they come. He has a button nose and a blazing smile. Spending time with Colin feels mature; his European ways make him fascinating. His wit is sharp, and his confidence is both charming and reassuring. He makes me laugh until my sides ache, and with him, I feel a sense of ease and security I hadn't known existed.

Soon, our dates become a regular part of my life. We explore local beach bars and nightlife, and spend countless hours at his apartment. Nestled on the hillside between Fuengirola and Mijas Pueblo, his apartment is a sanctuary of whitewashed walls, marble floors, and breathtaking views. One side overlooks the sparkling Mediterranean, the other the rugged beauty of the Andalusian mountains. We spend hours on the terrace, sharing meals, basking in the sun, losing ourselves in conversation. It is our private paradise, a place where time seems to slow down and worries fade away.

My life with Colin blossoms into a beautiful tapestry of shared experiences. Our relationship transcends the boundaries of romance, deepening into a profound and enduring connection. It feels like my first adult relationship.

"Do you want to go out to dinner Friday night?" Colin asks. I am surprised by this since he had made it clear at the beginning of our relationship that Friday nights were his nights out with his friends. I don't mind at all since I could also do something with my friends. However, Colin often lets me stay at his apartment while he is out.

"You are not going out with your friends?" I ask.

"I want to spend time with you," he replies in the soft voice he uses when I believe he is being vulnerable with me. Smiling, my heart warms to his words.

"Yes, of course, I would like that very much. I am surprised you are switching things up, but I am excited you want to spend that time with me," I say.

"Of course, Charly, you're my best friend, I always want to spend time with you," Colin says as he snuggles up to me on the couch. His vulnerability with me deepens my feelings for him. He has gone from someone too busy working to text me, to forgoing his weekly night out with friends to be with me.

We celebrate milestones together. Colin's father's wedding, a lavish affair on a steamboat cruising down the River Thames, is an unforgettable experience. And, of course, Colin reciprocates, visiting my family in the US, eager to experience a slice of my American life. But the visits to England became my cherished adventures. I fall in love with the English countryside, exploring quaint villages with Colin, meeting his family, and experiencing the unique rhythms of British life. Waking up in his father's house, there always seems to be someone having a tennis match. The sound of the tennis ball being volleyed was a quintessential English experience. I'll also never forget a thrilling ride in his father's vintage race car, a roaring journey through the rolling green hills that felt like something out of a movie.

After a year of this blissful relationship, I take the plunge and move in with him. Living with Colin is my first experience of living with a boyfriend. Colin takes great pride in his apartment. He has decorated it in a minimalist style. He makes space for me, and I feel at home in the apartment. Our days are filled with laughter at each other's quirks, the amusing cultural differences we encounter, and the often hilarious misunderstandings that arise from our attempts to navigate a world where even a shared language can sometimes feel like a foreign tongue. Our passion for each other is unstoppable. We explore our fantasies together.

One afternoon, the Andalusian sun was beating down, baking the terrace. We play a Moby CD, the rhythms pulsing a hypnotic counterpoint to the heat. Sweat beads on our skin, mingling with the scent of jasmine from the overflowing pots that lined the terrace walls.

"I'm going to grab a drink," I say, rising. "Anything for you?"

"Fanta lemon, please," Colin murmurs, shielding his eyes with a hand to look up at me. I smile, the heat making my skin feel alive.

Inside, the air is not a relief. There are no air conditioners here like in America. I stand at the refrigerator a minute longer than needed to feel its coolness on me. I return with two icy cans, straddling him where he lay, I playfully become a shadow against the blinding sunlight. Sitting up, he takes the Fanta, his eyes scrunching from the sun. I lower myself onto him, the heat between us intensifying. Leaning into him, I lay a slow, melting kiss on him that mirrors the languid rhythm of the afternoon, his hand sliding under my bikini top.

"Take this off," he growls. His hands, rough and urgent, tug the fabric from my shoulders. Colin lies back as I lean forward while taking off my suit. I offer myself to him, my breasts brushing against his lips as he claims it with a hungry kiss.

"Bite them," I whisper, my voice husky with desire. His teeth sink into my flesh, eliciting a sharp gasp. I feel him harden beneath me, a powerful surge against my thighs. Reaching down, I grip him through the fabric, urging him on. He breaks away from my breast, his eyes burning with a primal hunger. His shorts fall away, revealing him in all his glory. I guide him inside me, a deep, primal moan escaping my lips.

He thrusts upwards, his hands finding my hips, holding me captive. I ride him, a rhythmic dance of pleasure. The day's heat, the sun, and our bodies moving in unison create an intoxicating haze. Sweat drips down my back, mingling with the scent of our arousal.

"Harder," I plead, my voice breathless. "Bite my nipple." He obeys, his movements becoming faster, more urgent. I cry out, arching my back, lost in the ecstasy. A low groan rumbles from his throat, his body shuddering with release. We slow, our breathing ragged. I look down at him, a triumphant smile gracing my lips.

"Thanks, Chapstick," he teases, a mischievous glint in his eyes. I giggle, leaning down to kiss him.

"You're going to call me that now, are you?" I ask, playfully pushing him. I've never had anyone make up a nickname for me.

"Absolutely," he declares, grinning.

I slide off him, grabbing the towel I'd been lounging on. Looking back, I watch him pull on his shorts, taking a long sip of Fanta.

While cleaning up after dinner the night before, I'd casually mentioned needing some Chapstick.

"What's Chapstick?" he'd asked, completely bewildered.

"What do you mean, what is Chapstick? You've never heard of it?" I'd exclaimed. "It's that stuff you put on your lips when they're chapped!"

He looked thoughtful. "I know lip balm. There is a lip balm named Blistex. That you use for chapped lips."

That's when I realized. "In America," I'd explained, "Chapstick is a brand, but we call anything we put on our lips Chapstick, even if it's Blistex. There was a commercial from the '70s or '80s. With Olympic skier Susie Chapstick. She was skiing down the mountain, and she'd slide into the camera, showing off her Chapstick!" I'd mimed skiing, pretending to hold up a Chapstick.

Colin had burst out laughing. "Okay, Chapstick, I have never seen that commercial" he'd said, pulling me close for a hug. "You're my Susie Chapstick."

I dreamed of a future with Colin filled with bilingual children who would grow up speaking Spanish and English. I envisioned summers spent in the US, introducing our children to their American heritage. School breaks going to England to be a part of their British heritage. These idyllic dreams are fueled by love and a deep-seated desire to build a life together.

Living in Spain had broadened my horizons in ways I'd never imagined. My diverse circle of friends included English, Australian, Norwegian, and Persian backgrounds, each bringing a unique cul-

tural perspective to our interactions. I'd learned to appreciate the nuances of different cultures and understand that, despite our global political differences, as individuals, our world views are shaped by our unique experiences.

I'd also gained a valuable perspective on American culture. Living abroad allowed me to see my own country through a different lens. I'd realized that the rest of the world doesn't always view America through the same rose-colored glasses as many Americans do. This realization fostered a sense of humility and a deeper appreciation for the diverse and complex world around us. Ultimately, I'd learned that at the heart of every human experience lies a universal yearning for love, connection, and a meaningful life. Whether in Spain, England, the United States, or anywhere else in the world, the human spirit strives for happiness, connection, and a sense of belonging. In that shared human experience, I'd found a profound sense of unity and understanding.

At 28, I stand on the precipice of a life I never imagined, a life I built with nothing more than two suitcases and a reckless, exhilarating sense of adventure. My mother's warnings of you're making the biggest mistake of your life still echo in my ears. Some "friends" even placed bets on how quickly I'd return, their skepticism a bitter pill to swallow. But I'd done it. I'd left the familiar shores of America and embarked on a journey of self-discovery in Spain. There have been some challenges and lonely times. But these last two years I have grown, learned, and blossomed in ways I never could have imagined if I had stayed back home.

However, my path to legal residency in Spain was fraught with unexpected obstacles. Marriage to Colin seemed like the obvious solution. After all, we were deeply in love, our lives intertwined. Yet, when it came to marriage, our paths diverged. Colin had a fear of marriage. He'd watched his parents divorce and then divorce others. He was not *confident in the commitment of marriage, even if it was to secure my ability to stay with him in Spain.*

During our last visit to the US, he dropped a bombshell. He suggested I stay, hinting at a temporary separation. I naively assumed it was a logistical issue, a minor bump in the road. I believed he would call me, wanting me to return to Spain because he couldn't bear to be away from me. After all, that's how romantic comedies unfolded, wasn't it? But Colin didn't follow the script. He didn't just return to Spain; he broke up with me instead. After four months of living apart, he pulled off the band-aid.

"Chapstick, I think it is best we don't continue this relationship. The distance is too much." Colin cautiously said. His words sounded careful, as if he were speaking to me like I was a fragile mirror about to crack.

"Then I will come back, I will come back to Spain to be with you." I plead.

"I can't have that responsibility." He admitted. "I don't want you to be resentful towards me if you are not happy here."

"I would be happy, I am happy when I am with you. I now know that I won't have a career like I thought I would, or be surrounded by my friends. But as long as I am with you, I'll be ok." I cried, tears flooding my eyes, flowing down my cheeks.

"I'm sorry, Chapstick, you can't come back here, you can't."

"But, please."

"I'm sorry. I need to hang up. I will check on you in a day or so." He said.

"Please, Colin."

"Bye Chapstick." His voice is soft. Then I hear silence on the other end of the phone. I laid back on my bed, and curled my knees up to my chest, letting out sobs. Devastation washed over me and left me gasping for breath. He was supposed to come back for me. That is what the

movies show us - separate, so that he realizes how much he needs you, and then he shows up at your doorstep declaring his love.

Over the next six months, the realization that Colin and I would not be together began to settle in. I am angry at myself and my naiveté. I should have gone back with him. I should have fought harder and pleaded with him that I would be returning with him. Leaving him and Spain is a huge regret, a "what if" I can't let go of.

Charly & Jamie 1999

Standing on the porch of Glen Magna, my dad is beside me. "Cha, you ready?" he asks.

I watch my bridesmaids walk across the lawn to where everyone else is seated. Marie, the last one due to being my maid of honor, turns, smiles at me, and mouths "love you." I spot Jamie standing with his groomsmen beside them. "Pachelbel's Canon" begins to play, and everyone stands and turns toward me.

"Okay, Dad, here we go!"

"You can still run," my dad says and laughs.

"Not funny, Dad!" Together, we start walking down the aisle. I can see my mom crying her eyes out. I expected her to be even more of a mess than she is—she always cries at weddings, even ones on TV.

As I walk down the aisle toward Jamie, I look at him in his white tux with a black bowtie. I didn't think he could get more handsome, but seeing him in the tux, I can't believe I'm marrying this man. The love and adoration I feel for him overwhelms me. Each step I take toward him feels as though I am floating. I know I am here, but I also feel as though this is all a dream. I tighten my grip on my father's arm to ground myself.

He turns to me, smiles, and says, "you got this."

I look forward to Jamie again, and a sense of peace and contentment overcomes me; I know he is my person.

When I get to the altar, Jamie says, "You look radiant."

I smile at him and mouth, "I love you."

He says, "I love you."

The officiant sounds like the adults in the Charlie Brown cartoons, all muffled. Then I hear Jamie's voice, saying, "I look forward with great joy to spending the rest of my life with you."

Looking into his eyes, I repeat, "and I vow to be true and faithful. Today I give myself to you in marriage."

"Ladies and gentlemen, I introduce you to Mr. and Mrs. James and Charlene Walsh."

Jamie grabs my hand and raises it high over our heads as we face everyone. We are married; it went so fast, but it felt like slow motion. We dash down the aisle past our family and friends. For a quick moment, I wish we could keep going and leave everyone to celebrate alone somewhere.

The festivities start with an hour of taking photos. We do traditional family pictures and wedding party pictures. The photographer brings Jamie and me to the wrap-around porch of Glen Magna. As he positions us along the white columns and stairs, I'm so glad we have this time alone together. I keep looking at him, smiling, and I have to keep touching him to make sure this is not a dream.

"We have to make sure we eat," I tell Jamie because I'm starving. Jamie asks for a tray of appetizers and glasses of champagne.

"Here, eat some of these." He hands me some Spanakopitas and a glass of champagne. "Drink up! We're going to party!"

Looking at the tent filled with family and friends, it seems like a dream. Twinkling lights are everywhere, and white hydrangeas are centerpieces in tall glass columns. White linens cover the tables, and the chairs are white. It's magical.

"Wow, it looks beautiful in there."

I smile at Jamie and say, "I'm glad you like it. Now you know what all the arguing and crying with my mother was about." I laugh, and Jamie kisses my head.

"Thank you for making our wedding feel like a fairy tale," he says.

"Ladies and gentlemen, please stand for Mr. and Mrs. Walsh," we hear the DJ say.

As we walk into the tent, I laugh while everyone claps and cheers.

The night is everything I've dreamed my wedding would be. It feels like I've danced for hours with my friends, family, and Jamie. We danced to "All For Love" by Bryan Adams, Rod Stewart, and Sting as our wedding song. Jamie looks into my eyes while he lip-syncs the words of the song. I rest my head on his shoulder, close my eyes, and take a deep breath, knowing he will be mine forever to have and to hold.

By midnight, all the guests have left, and I am sitting at a table, exhausted. My feet ache despite taking off my shoes and wearing my Adidas flip-flops. I watch my mom and Jamie's mom walk around, gathering the centerpieces that are left.

"What are you going to do with those?" I ask them.

My mother says, "Oh, I'm putting one in the dining room and bringing the others to your grandmother and your aunts."

"I'll put one somewhere in my apartment and bring a couple to work," Sandy, Jamie's mom, says.

Jamie walks over to me, wearing only his tux pants and shirt, with the top three buttons unbuttoned.

"May I have this dance, Mrs. Walsh?" he asks, holding out his hand.

"The DJ is packing up," I say, nodding toward the musicians.

"We don't need music," Jamie replies, still holding out his hand. I take it, and Jamie embraces me, holding my hand to his heart, and begins to sway with me.

"I had the best day of my life so far, Charly. I know we have many more best days ahead, but I want to remember this one for a while," Jamie says, looking down at me.

"I am never going to forget this day," I tell him. He lifts my chin and kisses me softly.

"Thank you again for planning an amazing wedding. I am going to make you the happiest woman," Jamie murmurs as he lightly kisses my lips.

"I'm so happy it all went smoothly. I love you and wanted everything to be perfect for you." I exhale, " I am exhausted and ready to go home to bed," I reply. He continues to sway, dancing as if there were music playing.

"I need a few more minutes of this day," Jamie says. I let him have his moment, following his lead in our dancing.

"Okay, sweetie, let's get you home. But I hope you're not too tired because I need a few hours to consummate this marriage," he says.

"I've been waiting for this part of our wedding day all day!" I exclaim, standing on my toes to be at eye level with him. We share a kiss that feels like our first.

"Come on, Mrs. Walsh, we'd better get home before I fuck you right here on the dance floor," Jamie says as we turn to walk out of the tent.

Hearing the alarm, I can feel the pounding in my head before I open my eyes. My mouth feels like a desert. We are flying to our honeymoon this afternoon. Lying here, hungover, I find myself questioning why I agreed to take a flight the day after our wedding. I feel Jamie turning over and coming closer to me. He wraps his arm around me and pulls me in to spoon with him.

"I am so hungover," I whisper.

"Me too. You know what's a good cure for a hangover?" Jamie asks.

"You getting me some Tylenol, a Brisk Iced Tea, and Saltines," I reply. Then, I can feel Jamie's hand sliding down my naked body. I can also feel him getting harder against me. "I am hungover," I say to him, knowing what he wants right now.

"You don't have to do anything," he says as he slides his hand across my hip and between my legs and begins to rub me. With his other hand, he reaches under me and massages my breast. He knows I melt and am ready to go when he touches my breast. We stay spooned as our bodies move in a rhythm of pleasure.

Lying there for a moment, our bodies still intertwined, he whispers, "Good morning, Mrs. Walsh."

"Good morning," I reply, rolling over to look at him. "That was a fantastic way to start the day as a married couple. Can we always begin the day like that?"

"Well, I was thinking this is how we're starting our honeymoon, but yes, we can start every day that way." He winks as he gets out of bed. "Okay, Mrs. Walsh, let's shake off these hangovers to continue our honeymoon. Next stop: Aruba." Jamie walks out of the room.

My parents gifted us their timeshare, and Jamie and I decided to go to Aruba for our honeymoon. Our flight leaves in five hours, which gives us plenty of time to recover from this hangover and get to the airport. Jamie returns with Saltines and a bottle of Tylenol. He hands me the crackers, shakes out two pills, and gives them to me. I grab the water from my bedside, swallow the pills, and place a Saltine on my tongue to dissolve.

"Watch out, world! The Walshes are coming!" Jamie shouts. *The Walshes,* I say to myself. *I am a wife.*

Millennium

Charly & Jamie 2001

Sitting at my desk at work, my heart pounds when an AOL Instant Message from Melissa popped up: "A plane just flew into the World Trade Center in NYC." *Strange*, I thought, but also, considering how tall they were, it was not unimaginable. My friendship with Melissa had continued after our days waitressing at Supino's. We were constantly messaging on AOL, now at our full-time jobs. Melissa had gone into marketing and works at a computer software company.

I glance around the bustling gym of the Jewish Community Center. No one seemed alarmed, oblivious to what was unfolding. I hurry to the TVs, my eyes scanning the screens. As I drew closer to the TVs, my breath caught in my throat. The Twin Towers were engulfed in smoke.

"What's happening?" I ask another gym member, my voice trembling. I had been hoping Melissa had been wrong.

"Two planes... flew into them," he replies, his face pale.

The gravity of the situation begins to set in with me, and a cold dread creeps into my bones. I can't comprehend the scale of the disaster, its sheer brutality. More members abandon their workouts, drawn to the horrifying spectacle unfolding before them. Back in the office, I dial Jamie's office number, my hand shaking.

"Have you seen what's happening in NYC?" My voice is barely a whisper when he picks up.

"No, I've been buried at my desk," he says, his voice laced with confusion. "Why, what happened?"

I recount the events, my voice trembling as I describe the scenes of chaos and destruction.

"Let me talk to some people here. I'll call you back," Jamie says, his voice now tinged with alarm.

Returning to the fitness room, I find myself surrounded by faces etched with grief and disbelief. A woman sobs, saying, "I have family in New York City."

As the day unfolds, the news paints a terrifying picture of a co-ordinated terrorist attack. Three planes took off from Boston, their paths converging on a single, horrific objective. Our Executive Director announces an early dismissal, a sense of unease permeating the center.

Driving home, the radio is only news reports of the details of the tragedy unfolding in chilling detail. A heavy silence descends, and a palpable sense of fear hangs in the air.

"I'm home," I say, my voice small through the phone at our apartment. I realized I still had my keys in my hand and my work bag on my shoulder as I stood in our kitchen. I had been in such a rush to call him as soon as I got home.

"They might let us go soon. I'll call you," he says, his voice strained. Jamie's office is in Gloucester; if he does leave, it would only take him thirty minutes to get home.

"It's so quiet outside," I say, panic rising in my chest. "What if there are more attacks?"

"I know, it's terrifying," he says. "I'll be home as soon as I can. Love you."

"Hurry home, I love you."

Finally, the sound of the front door opening brings a wave of relief to me. Jamie's embrace is comfort in the face of the unknown.

"This is the scariest thing that has ever happened to our country, in our lifetime," he whispers, holding me close.

"Jamie," I begin, my voice hesitant, "I have something to tell you... and it's probably the worst timing, but I had planned to tell you today."

He looks at me, his eyes wide with confusion. "What is it?"

"I'm pregnant."

A wave of anxiety washes over me. Would he be happy? Would he be scared?

"What?" he breathes, his eyes searching mine.

"I know it's not ideal," I rush on, "but I took a test yesterday, and it was positive. I need to make a doctor's appointment, but with everything that's happening..."

"Charly," he says, his voice gentle, "shh. I'm glad you told me. I wasn't expecting this news, but... I'm excited! This is amazing."

He pulls me close, saying, "How long have you suspected? What made you take the test? I have so many questions!"

"You're not mad?" I ask, still hesitant.

"Why would I be? It feels strange to be celebrating amidst all this... but I am happy," he says, his voice filled with wonder.

We eat dinner in front of the television; the news reports a grim backdrop to our newfound joy.

"9/11," Jamie says, "we'll never forget this day."

"For many reasons," I say, a tear rolling down my cheek. He kisses me tenderly.

"Thank you," he whispers.

Charly & Jamie 2002

"Jamie, wake up." I shake Jamie, sleeping next to me. "Jamie!" He rolls over. "I'm having strong contractions."

"Crap. Okay, what do you want to do?" Jamie sits up, looking at me.

"I don't know. Should we call the hospital?"

"You're the one having a baby!" he sputters.

"I know, but I can't think straight right now." I start tearing up. I don't like others making decisions for me, but right now, I need Jamie to do what I often don't let him do.

"Okay, I'll call the hospital. You start getting yourself ready in case they say we should come in," Jamie says.

As I get out of bed, another contraction hits. I double over, holding my stomach, and yell as the pain rises. I can't hold back the tears. I'm scared, and it hurts so badly. I don't want to do this anymore.

"How far apart are the contractions?" Jamie looks at me holding the phone. Looking up at him as I am bent over the bed, I look him straight in the eyes.

"Uhm, I don't think she knows at the moment," he says into the receiver.

"Tell them they are about 45 minutes apart," I manage to mumble as I bite the sheets.

"Okay, ah uh...okay...they said we should head on in." He comes over, kisses the top of my head, and looks into my eyes. "Everything will be okay. I will do whatever I can to make this as smooth as possible."

I continue to cry and say, "You have no idea how painful this is, and I don't want to do it."

Jamie laughs, "Well, you have to. There's no choice. Try to breathe as we learned in Lamaze class."

"Go fuck yourself," I tell him. He laughs.

"Ah, there's my Boston girl. I thought I lost her when she graduated and stopped going into the city. I will grab the bags and help you to the car," he patiently says.

I chose to deliver at Beverly Hospital in Beverly, MA. That's where my family has gone for everything. It was a 20-minute drive from our apartment. Just as we get on the highway, another contraction hits. I hope Jamie doesn't crash as I yell through it. He grabs my hand as I settle back, reminding me to breathe. Forget breathing. Forget what the Lamaze teacher said. I'll do whatever I want right now. I know how to take care of myself and what I need. Jamie assures me he will call my parents and his mom.

"Wait until we know this is real. What if these are just Braxton hicks?" I didn't want everyone rushing up for no reason.

When I arrive at the emergency room, they admit me quickly. As the nurse helps me onto the bed, I feel relief between my legs. Crap. "Ugh, I'm sorry, I peed," I say to the nurse.

"No, honey. Your water broke," the nurse says, patting me on the shoulder. "It looks like you're having your baby."

Jamie hasn't come in from parking the car yet. Thank goodness, I didn't want him to see me like this. I know he loves me no matter what, but there are some things I don't think he needs to know. He may never find me sexy again. The nurse gets me settled in the bed, and just then Jamie comes in while she hooks me up to the IVs. His eyes widen when he sees her injecting me.

"We're having a baby," I say to him.

Jamie pulls a chair to the bedside, takes my hand, and says, "You got this," before kissing me. It's 2:30 am, my Grandma Carlen's birthday. I rub my stomach and plead, "Please, baby, arrive today. Grandma will be so happy."

"The doctor is on his way. If you get thirsty, here are some ice chips. If you have a contraction, Dad, watch the time. We will transport you to the delivery room shortly," the nurse instructs before leaving.

"It's the middle of the night. Don't call your mom or my parents until after 6 am," I tell Jamie. "And we are good with the names we agreed on?"

"James William if it's a boy, Cari Carol if it's a girl," Jamie replies. We'd decided not to find out what we were having. I decorated the baby's room in yellow and soft green. My mom and Susan wanted to help me set it up, but I had the picture in my mind of what I wanted, and I wanted to do it myself. I did let Jamie set up the crib, which ended up being a test of our relationship.

James William, Jamie's junior, was born at 12:37 PM on Tuesday, May 26, 2002, weighing 8 lbs 10 oz. I'm exhausted. The delivery was awful, and I never want to go through that again. I keep asking everyone if I can please sleep. The nurses keep telling me I need to stay awake a little longer. My family is here, and everyone is gushing over James, whom we will be calling JJ. Plenty of people are around to care for him, so I should be able to sleep. Finally, I get the okay from the doctor to rest. When I wake up two hours later, I still feel groggy, as if I could sleep for another 12 hours.

"Mom, we need to get some food for you," a nurse says as she sets a tray on the table over my bed.

"I just want to sleep," I reply.

"I know, but you'll get used to being tired," she smiles. I don't see anything to smile about with that statement.

"Where is my husband?" I ask.

"He went home to shower. He said he would be back as fast as he could." *How lucky for him,* I think.

"Can I take a shower?" I ask the nurse.

"Of course, but let's get some food first to give you strength. We also need to start feeding the baby. Then we will get you showered," the nurse says.

I'd decided to breastfeed. The hospital provides a lactation nurse who helps JJ and me. I enjoy this time with JJ as he cuddles up to me, and I provide him with nutrients. I love holding his little fingers. Jamie sits on the edge of the bed while I feed JJ, watching us.

"You are so beautiful," Jamie tells me.

"I'm a mess. My hair is matted and so dirty," I say to Jamie.

"I don't care about that. Watching you and seeing how your body provides for our son makes me so happy. We have a human all our own," he says, laughing.

Our transition into parenthood is a rollercoaster. Thank goodness for Sandy, Jamie's mom. Although my mom is helpful, Sandy is a nurse who took two weeks off to stay with us and help with everything I can imagine. I've become dependent on her. Sandy made lunch for us this afternoon while JJ fell asleep after his late morning feeding. She and I are sitting at the kitchen table when I suddenly start crying.

"Oh, Charly, what is it?" Sandy sympathetically asks.

"I don't think I can do everything, and I'm not going to be able to do everything as well as you," I say through tears.

"I appreciate you thinking I can do everything. I've done this once before. No one expects you to do everything or do it perfectly," Sandy assures me.

"I feel such pressure to be a good wife, to raise a child so he doesn't turn out to be an awful person, and to be myself. I'm not even sure I know who I am right now." I feel relieved to say all that. It's been weighing on my mind. Over the years, Sandy has become someone I can confide in, and I feel lucky to have her as my mother-in-law.

Sandy tells me I have a fantastic support system, but that I need to accept it. She reminds me that I often push away support and help. I'm surprised to hear her say this. She must have seen the surprise on my face because she tells me that Jamie has expressed frustrations to her about me not accepting help.

"People are not mind readers and want to help, especially Jamie, your parents, and me. Let us help and support you," she says. I promise her I will. I also promise to do my best to give her son and grandson the best life possible.

Charly 2003

*O*nce again, I move out of my parents' house, hopefully for the final time. I'd answered an ad on apartment.com listed by two professional women in Charlestown, Melissa and Tracey. Moving to Charlestown marks a new chapter on my journey back to myself from the heartbreak of my breakup with Colin. It is still a shadow that occasionally darkens my days, but I am learning to live with it more slowly.

Honestly, therapy has been a lifeline in this whole healing thing. It's where I'm slowly realizing I actually have a voice, a choice in how things go. For so long, I felt like I was living life according to this plan society handed me—what I should be doing, who I should be. I once believed that I needed a guy to choose me in order to feel worthy and validated. Looking back at my relationships, I so desperately wanted them to want me, to choose me. I don't think I realized that they were by being with me. I always felt as though I needed to keep proving myself worthy of being in the relationships. As if they would see the real me and not want to be with me. I have been going through life seeking external validation when I should have been validating myself. It's only now that I'm starting to figure out what I want. The other day in therapy, I started really digging into that. I found myself saying out loud, almost surprised, "I know, eventually, I picture myself getting married. But right now... it just doesn't feel like it's important."

My therapist (she's good) just gently asked, "What's making you say that, Charly?"

And I just spilled, "I don't know if it's the fear of getting hurt again, or if something's really shifting inside me, but I just don't feel that desperate need to find a guy and live that whole 'happily ever after' thing I used to think I wanted. It almost feels... superficial to me right now," I admitted.

She just nodded like she understood." 'That makes sense,' she said, "you've been disappointed, and maybe that disappointment is showing you that there's more to life than what you initially believed." Hearing her say it like that was a relief. It felt good, really good, to finally say out loud that I don't need a relationship as much as I thought. That I'd actually be okay on my own.

Finally living in the city opens up a whole new world of possibilities. Suddenly, my social circle explodes. I am meeting other thirty-something single women in my neighborhood and at work. I work as an assistant to a financial advisor at a firm in downtown Boston, which leads to many after-work happy hours and tickets to sports games. I now have a growing network of friends in Boston. My weekend schedule is also being filled with activities: brunch dates, bars, and impromptu shopping excursions around the city. It's the quintessential urban experience with a vibrant tapestry of friendships and fleeting romances.

Getting back into the dating game is interesting. I try to have fun with it. There seems to be the continued inevitable dating adventures, a revolving door of charming men, each with his unique brand of charisma. I jokingly call myself a "one-date wonder," because I wonder why I don't get a second or third date.

Following the women on "Sex and the City", I give nicknames to my dates. Take Mr. Vice, oh, he was fun! I'd met him through a mutual friend, and we'd gone on two dates. He was so handsome, physically everything I could have hoped for and more. He lived two streets away from me. On our first date, we went to a noodle bar and then to a laser show. On the second date, we went to dinner in our neighborhood, then grabbed a bottle of wine and two glasses and headed up to his rooftop. While sipping wine, looking out at the Boston skyline, he glanced over at me.

"I don't know what will happen with us," he says, "but I do know that I am happy getting to know you. I feel great about us."

Well, this is promising, I thought to myself, hearing his words. A week later, after not hearing from him, I got the "sorry, I got busy, I am not in a place to do this with you right now" text.

Then came Mr. Penthouse. I met him out of the blue at a bar on a Friday night. He just walked right up and started asking me all sorts of questions. I didn't even know if he was with anyone. He asked for my number, and I gave it, though honestly, I didn't expect to hear from him and wouldn't have been disappointed if I hadn't. He seemed a little tipsy, but his friends, who eventually joined our conversation, kept insisting he was a great guy. Two nights later, a text popped up from an unknown number. It was almost poetic: 'those lips, those eyes, they took me by surprise.' I thought it was a wrong number. When I replied with 'Who is this?' and got back 'Mr. Penthouse,' I was intrigued. He asked me out for the following Friday, making reservations at Prezza, the best spot in the North End, and coincidentally owned by someone I had gone to high school with. Seeing him again that Friday, I was struck by how handsome he was—I'd genuinely forgotten. Over dinner, it became clear that he was very wealthy. The expensive restaurant was the first clue. Then he mentioned his family's time at the Breakers in Florida and that he lived in an apartment at the corner of Arling-

ton and Beacon Streets—the heart of Back Bay, where only the well-off reside. Beyond the apparent wealth, I genuinely enjoyed his company. We had a good conversation, easy banter, and a lot of laughter. After dinner, he drove me home, kissed me goodnight, said he'd enjoyed our evening, and that he'd be in touch soon. I never heard from him again.

Mr. Mayer, I have a pretty good idea of what went down there. We met at The Harp. We were chatting, and then when 'Your Body is a Wonderland' came on, he absolutely insisted we had to dance to it. As we were swaying along, Tracy walked by and said something, and without thinking, I jokingly blurted out, 'I am marrying this man!' The following weekend, Mr. Mayer and I went for dinner at a restaurant in the Prudential building. Afterwards, we headed downstairs to another bar, where I unfortunately had one too many drinks and ended up quite drunk. The next morning, nursing a truly epic hangover and sitting miserably on the edge of my bed, my roommate Tracy walked past my room.

"Eek, you look awful! How was your date last night?"

"I feel awful, so clearly it was fun." But honestly, the end of the night is a complete blur, and I had no idea if I'd ever hear from him again. I didn't. Which I took to mean he was not impressed with how much I drank that night.

But I refuse to let disappointment define me. I keep my heart open, believing the right person will come along eventually. Someone who will truly see me for who I am, with all my quirks and flaws. Someone who will cherish me, protect me, and love me fiercely. Someone who will be not just my lover but my best friend. I told my therapist that I was not in a rush.

My friendships were what kept me grounded and thriving. Marie, who is still my closest friend, shocked me with the news that she and her family decided to move to Houston. Marie married Matt, a *guy she met in her mid-twenties, and they have two children. I adore Jack and Rene.*

"You can't move!" I say, tears welling up in my eyes.

"Why?" she asks.

"Because you can't leave me," I tell her, finally acknowledging the extent of my dependence on her.

"You left me when you moved to Spain," Marie gently reminds me. The silence that follows is deafening. Her words strike a chord, a painful reminder of the hurt I'd inflicted on others while chasing my dreams.

This theme appears with my mother as well. She truly thought I was ruining my life by going to Spain. I didn't mean to hurt anyone with my choices for myself, especially not Marie. However, with my mother, it felt like a direct challenge to my autonomy.

Yet, amidst the sadness of Marie moving, new friendships blossom through my work and through meeting new people in the city. I reconnect with Asher, the guy I had a crush on back in my early twenties when he worked at Kelly's Roast Beef. He is as handsome and charming as I remember. Dating him felt like a playful throwback to my teenage years, although it only lasted about six months.

Weddings become a recurring theme in my life. Many of my friends from Danvers are getting married. As a bridesmaid, I stand by their sides, my heart swelling with joy as I witness them embark on their marital adventures. Some friends who married young are now having baby showers, a celebration of a new life and a reminder of the incredible capacity for love and joy that exists in the world. Watching my friends navigate motherhood and their transformation fills me with profound awe and admiration.

Although I didn't return to working in the fitness industry after returning from Spain, I continued to pursue my passion for fitness, maintaining a gym membership and a regular workout routine. Cur-

rently, I have a gym membership at World Gym Somerville, near my Charlestown apartment. It is my daily therapy; it helps me stay connected to myself. It is the one constant thing in my life that I hold onto.

A perk at the company I work at is getting your birthday as a paid day off. Getting to sleep in on a weekday, on my birthday, is the best thing a job could give me. I wake up to the apartment smelling of the coffee brewing in the kitchen, waiting for me, thanks to my roommate. I decide to get to the gym for a late morning workout.

The familiar scent of iron and sweat fills the air as I slide my membership card through the scanner.

"Happy Birthday!" The young guy working at the front desk says to me. A look of surprise must have been on my face when I glanced at him. "It comes up on the computer when you slide your card." He laughs.

"Oh, thank you." I smile at him. World Gym Somerville holds a certain nostalgic charm, reminding me of the energetic atmosphere of Nautilus Plus back in my hometown. I spent most of my twenties working out at Nautilus Plus.

Looking around the gym, I see a familiar face walking toward me in a police uniform. Peter Finley. Time seems to freeze. It's been years since our breakup. I haven't thought of him in a long time. The way our relationship ended became an unexpected lesson, gently guiding me to understand that life's path often veers from our expectations. Although I admit I reacted too quickly in breaking up with him. But I hadn't, I wouldn't have gone to Spain. I would never have had that experience in my life.

Reflecting on it now, my parting with Peter marked my first true foray into the complexities of adult relationships and their endings. Navigating the healing process revealed a strength within me I hadn't fully recognized before—the inner resolve to not settle for a partnership where investment wasn't mutual. This experience, though painful, ultimately illuminated my capacity for self-respect and the courage to seek relationships with people who truly nurture and value me.

"Peter Finley," I say, a wave of unexpected warmth washing over me. "How are you?" He is as handsome as ever. He is still styling his blond hair like an outgrown buzzcut. I forgot how blue his eyes are.

"Charly Carlsen," he says, a hint of a smile playing on his lips. "I'm a Somerville police officer now."

"Well, that is good to hear; otherwise, I would find it awfully strange of you to be wearing their uniform. Good for you, that is awesome," I exclaim, genuinely impressed.

"Don't let me see you getting into trouble that I need to get you out of," he teases, shining his smile that made my heart flutter. I smile, remembering how he loved to tease me and give me a hard time.

"Don't worry, I won't dream of it," I say.

"I've got to go. It was great seeing you, Charly." Peter leans into me, hugging me. I'd missed the feeling of standing on my tiptoes, hugging him.

I feel a strange sense of peace watching him walk out the doors. The encounter was brief, yet there was no awkwardness, no lingering resentment. It was as if we had picked up where we left off, two friends catching up after a long absence.

Thinking about our relationship and how it ended, I realize that perhaps our paths were meant to diverge. We were better as friends, two classmates who had admired and supported each other.

The September air crackles with excitement. My friend Tonya, a vibrant Portuguese beauty I work with, is moving back to California. We decide to do a final weekend in New York City.

The bus ride was a blur of anticipation. Port Authority Bus Terminal, a chaotic symphony of human movement, is our first encounter in New York.

"I am getting a hot dog as soon as we get out of here. I am starving, I could have eaten the arm of a bus chair," I say to Tonya as we both laugh. "I don't know why we did not pack snacks for a four-hour ride."

Once we get a hot dog from a street vendor, we navigate through the maze of streets. Tonya's itinerary includes getting cosmopolitans, of course.

"Just like on 'Sex and the City,'" Tonya says with excitement in her eyes.

We make our way to Mulberry Street for Italian food for dinner. We wander along the busy streets after dinner, looking for a bar. We encounter a line of people waiting to get into what looks like a club, but with no window, we could not tell. Tonya, ever the intrepid explorer, approaches the bouncer.

"What's this place?" she asks. A spark of recognition ignited in his eyes.

"Eres portuguesa?" he asks, a knowing smile playing on his lips. A brief exchange in their native dialect, leaving Tonya beaming.

"Who are you with?" he asks, surveying the scene.

"My friend," she replies, gesturing toward me.

With a flourish, he puts wristbands on us. "VIP area," he instructs, "through those doors." He points to doors down a hall as he opens the door of the club.

The club was a sensory overload—low-hanging lights casting an ethereal glow, a throbbing beat pulsing through the air. A tray of shimmering cocktails in martini glasses passes by.

"Those," Tonya declares, pointing.

"Come on, let's go to the bar and get you a cosmo. I will buy the first round." I insist.

Glancing around the room, taking in the different people, my eyes land on a guy. Standing across the room, a vision in black—a simple T-shirt, a sharp blazer, and hair that shined black—our eyes meet, a fleeting moment that sends a jolt through me. I quickly avert my gaze, pretending not to notice, though my heart hammers against my ribs.

Oblivious to my internal turmoil, Tonya spots an empty booth up for grabs. But my gaze keeps returning to him. Every time I look, it feels like he is watching me, too.

"Hey," I whisper to Tonya, "there's this guy... he's... wow."

"Go talk to him," Tonya urges.

"No way," I exclaim, blushing.

"Let me go see what's up," Tonya says, a true wing girl in action.

She approaches the group of men, her gaze darting back to me for confirmation. I nod, my stomach doing a nervous flip-flop. Returning to the table, she whispers, "They're coming over!"

"What did they say?" I ask, breathless.

"I don't know," she says, "I just told them to come over." And then he stood before me, a mesmerizing figure with dark, captivating eyes.

"Hi," he says, his voice a deep tone.

"Hi," I reply, my voice trembling slightly.

His friend, Ardit, introduces himself.

"I'm Charly," I say, extending a hand to Ardit.

Finally, it was the mysterious man's turn. "I'm Dardan," he says, his gaze unwavering. "I saw you looking at me."

My breath hitches. "I... I was looking at you because you were looking at me," I stammer, feeling a blush creep up my neck.

He chuckles, a low, melodious sound. "Oh, is that how it was?"

"Seems that way," I retort, a playful smile gracing my lips.

"Do you live in NYC?" he asks.

"No, I'm from Boston," I say, a fleeting worry crossing my mind.

"Never been to Boston," he says.

"Well," I say, flashing a smile, "maybe I can help you find a reason to visit."

His dark and intense eyes hold mine captive. "Perhaps you can," he murmurs, a slow, seductive smile spreading across his face.

The night swirls into a dizzying mix of laughter, witty banter, and stolen glances. I learn that Ardit and Dardan are Albanian, which somehow makes them even more intriguing. Dardan works in IT and lives in Brooklyn, while Ardit calls Astoria, Queens, home.

"We're heading to French Toast for some food; it is an all-night dinner," Ardit announces. "You ladies want to join?"

I exchange a quick glance with Tonya, my eyes widening with silent approval.

"I'm game for all the adventures," Tonya declares, her eyes sparkling with excitement.

And so, the adventure continues. The French Toast reminds me of a café in the North End. Dardan got escargot, which I find to be an odd choice after a night of drinking. After the delicious meal at the diner, Ardit suggests heading back to his place in Astoria. A wave of hesitation washes over me. We are in a strange city, and this feels impulsive. Standing outside on the sidewalk, the city is still lively with people walking by, taxi after taxi passing, their horns honking. I look at Tonya; her eyes are glazed over, the effects of the cocktails finally catching up to her.

"Are you ok, do you want to go, or do you want to go back to the hotel?" I ask her, turning myself so the guys can't hear us.

"We came to have an adventure, I think this is it. Plus, you like that guy, right?" She encourages me.

"Ok, but if either one of us feels like we should go, we go." I look at her to agree.

"The code word is go." She smiles.

"Yeah, we can do that," I say to the guys as I turn, a small smile playing on my lips as I meet Dardan's gaze. "You okay with that?" I ask him.

"Sure," he says, a hint of a smile gracing his lips. "It'll be fun."

Ardit's apartment was a quintessential Queens: a heavy door secured with multiple locks and a long hallway leading to the living room. He gently ushers Tonya into the bedroom, returning moments later with sheets and pillows to set up the pull-out couch.

"She's already out cold," he says, a chuckle rumbling in his chest as we finish setting up the couch. "I'm going to hit the hay." With a nod, he walks back to the bedroom, leaving us alone.

Dardan begins to shed his shoes, then his pants. I follow suit, kicking off my shoes and leaving my dress on. As I climb into bed beside him, the room spins slightly, the effects of the alcohol starting to take hold. He lay beside me, our gazes meeting. Slowly, he reaches out, his hand brushing the side of my face. My breath hitches as he leans closer, his eyes darkening with a primal intensity. Then, his lips meet mine, a soft, exploratory touch that ignites a fire within me. I surrender to the passion that is rising in me. His hands, large on my body, slide under my dress, finding my breast. What am I doing? He is a stranger, I think in a moment of clarity.

"We need to stop," I whisper to him.

"Of course. Sleep well." Dardan says, pulling back.

"Good night," I whisper, rolling over. Sleep eludes me. Anxiety is creeping into my mind. I am sharing a bed with a stranger in a stranger's apartment in Astoria, Queens. Charly, you've gotten yourself into some crazy situations, but this takes the cake.

I must drift off eventually because the morning sun is already blazing through the window when I open my eyes. He is still asleep beside me, looking incredibly handsome, even in slumber. Those eyelashes! I swear, women would kill for lashes like that. It seems unfair that someone who clearly doesn't care about such things is blessed with such a magnificent feature. I realize I don't remember his name. I frantically search for a clue. I could check his license... if he even has one. Most Manhattanites don't drive, I'd heard. Of course, he has an ID. I am being silly. I sit up, my eyes darting around the room.

"Morning," Ardit's voice startles me.

"Morning," I reply, "is Tonya okay?"

"Yeah, she's coming," he says.

"Hi, morning," Tonya's voice croaks as she emerges from the bedroom, looking like a true walk of shame.

"I'll drive you ladies back to the hotel," Ardit offers. I notice he is already dressed and ready to go.

"Should we wake him?" I ask, gesturing next to me.

"Dardan," Ardit calls out loudly.

"Mmmm, I'm awake," Dardan mumbles, "all this talking, who can sleep?" Dardan. Dardan. I will remember his name.

Ardit pulls up in front of the hotel. "All right, ladies," he says.

"Thank you so much," I say, gathering my belongings. "It was great meeting you both."

Dardan leans over and kisses me, a lingering touch that sends a shiver down my spine.

"Put your number in my phone. I will text you to make sure you get back to Boston safely," he says. He hands me his phone, and I put in my phone number. I smile, handing it back to him as I get out of the car.

"Bye, guys!" Tonya calls out, leaning back from the door as Dardan approaches her to get in the passenger seat. As we watch the car

disappear down the street, Tonya and I look at each other and burst into laughter.

"What was that?" she gasps, shaking her head.

"I don't know," I admit, "but it was definitely an adventure."

We walk into the hotel, still giggling, two sleep-deprived, slightly disheveled girls who just had the most unexpected and exhilarating night in New York City. What a night to remember.

"Do you think he will text?" Tonya asks as we step into the elevator, pressing our floor number.

"I have no idea," I whisper, not wanting the other people in the elevator to hear.

"Do you want him to?" Tonya asks in a whisper.

The elevator dings, and the doors open to our floor, and we walk down the hall to our room.

"I don't know? I mean, he lives here, what could come of anything? I am not into long-distance relationships," I think to myself, especially after Colin. I stop at our room door, searching around in my purse for the key. Tonya reaches around me with her key and unlocks the door.

"Well, at least text back if he does contact you," Tonya encourages. "You never know what can happen."

"Hhmm, I will. You're right. You never know." My words may have sounded optimistic, but I was doubtful.

Charly & Jamie 2004

Though delightful, JJ's second birthday party lacked the grandeur of his first, the extravagant celebration hosted by my parents and mother-in-law. By Memorial Day, however, we had achieved a milestone of our own: we had finally moved into our dream home. Nestled within Woodvale, one of my favorite neighborhoods in Danvers, our new residence offers a glimpse into the life we are building together.

Woodvale, a 1950s-built neighborhood bordering the local middle and high school, is a tapestry of charming ranch-style homes, each a testament to the baby boom era. These classic "slab houses," built over the marshland, hold a special place in my heart. Growing up, I walked these very streets because my parents' house is located just outside the Woodvale perimeter. Most of my friends lived in Woodvale, so I would often walk to their houses. One of my memories of Woodvale homes is the electric heated floors. I'd had many sleepovers at friends' houses, where I would sweat in my sleeping bag from the heat.

Finding this house had been a stroke of serendipity. The allure of more space, the promise of a backyard for our growing family, and the undeniable appeal of the highly regarded Danvers school system ultimately swayed Jamie.

Before settling in, we embarked on a comprehensive renovation project, transforming the master bedroom and bathroom into spaces that reflect our evolving tastes and aspirations. As for other areas in the house, I wanted an open concept to have a view of the kitchen, dining area, and living room. Due to the structure of the house, Jamie is only able to knock down a few walls to create an open kitchen and dining area, with a small seating area that he told me could serve as my reading nook. Leaving us with a large living room leading into a screened-in porch with sliding glass doors. We both agree on neutral colors. Jamie is honing his skills through his successful house-flipping ventures, which have turned into his, or I should say, our thriving company, Walsh Construction. His keen eye for detail ensures our home will be a testament to our shared vision. We both want our home to be comfortable and minimalist at the same time.

After the party, I lay on the couch, exhausted, watching Jamie and JJ play with some of his new toys. Jamie seems to enjoy them, perhaps even more than JJ. Suddenly, a wave of nausea hits me, and I jump up from the couch. Realizing I won't reach the bathroom, I run to the sink. I hear Jamie yell, "Are you okay?" then I hear JJ, in his sweet voice, ask, "You k?"

"I don't know," I reply, standing over the sink, waiting to see if I will get sick again. I walk back into the room and lie down on the couch.

"I haven't felt this crappy since...."

"Since when?" Jamie asked, and JJ echoed, "s when?"

"Since I was pregnant with JJ," I say, looking at Jamie.

"Could you be pregnant?" Jamie asks.

"I sure could be," I say.

Jamie and I want another child, and we haven't been using any birth control. We'd decided to enjoy our sex life, and if we got pregnant, then it was meant to be. Our sex life has been better than ever in the past few months, likely due to the excitement of his thriving business and the completion of our house renovations. We both were eager for our family to grow.

I go and buy a pregnancy test to take the following day. Driving to CVS, I know I am pregnant. I understand my body, and I have been feeling exhausted lately. I just hadn't stopped to consider what was happening. Getting sick was my body's way of telling me to pay attention. As I sat in the car, I could feel it. My breasts felt swollen. I plan to take the test to show Jamie, since he would appreciate the confirmation.

The next day, Jamie nudges me awake, reminding me to take the test before he leaves for work. He usually leaves about an hour before JJ, and I do. I take JJ to daycare at the JCC, where I continue to work. I am now the director of the fitness center. I have focused on mental health and body confidence within the fitness center, rather than just weight loss or sports conditioning, just as I had dreamed of doing in college.

I drag myself out of bed to take the pregnancy test. I am exhausted, another sign that I am pregnant. Jamie goes to attend to JJ, who is calling us. Jamie returns to the room. I'm holding the test as I come out of the bathroom.

"So?" he asks, looking at the test in my hand. I smile.

"We're having another baby," I tell him. He hugs me with one arm while JJ is in the other.

"Fuck, yeah! Charly, this is amazing. Thank you for giving me the best life I could ever ask for." Jamie looks at JJ and says, "You will be a big brother."

I look at JJ, who has no idea what this means.

"I am going to make sure you are the best big brother," I tell JJ. He squirms in Jamie's arms and tries to escape them.

Putting JJ down, Jamie says we should call out of work today and stay home in bed all day. He puts his arms around me.

"Remember how we would stay in bed all weekend, having sex over and over again when we were first living together. Those were the best days." He whispers in my ear as he rubs his nose and lightly kisses my neck.

I felt so amazing back then. Jamie would gush over my body and touch every inch of it over and over. He couldn't get enough of me. I felt so sexy and admired. Not that he doesn't make me feel good now. I haven't felt good in my body since having JJ. I've always struggled with my weight. After having JJ, my body changed, and I am having a harder time managing my weight. Plus, I am so tired and busy that I don't get to work out the way I used to. Jamie is so handsome, and his body is so muscular. He gets to work out daily. My desire and lust for him help me let go of my insecurity for him to make love to me whenever he or I want. But I don't see my body as desirable; it's almost as if, since JJ was born, my body is not solely mine anymore.

"As much as I want you to throw me down on the bed." I glance at the bed. Jamie follows my glance with his eyes, widening. "And have wild, crazy sex. We can't. I can't call out, and you have our company to run." I remind him.

He responds with, "I know it wouldn't be appropriate to set JJ up in the living room alone while I devour you." We both laugh, embrace, and tease each other with touches.

I pull away, pushing him a little. "Get ready for work. I am going to shower quickly before you leave."

"I'll watch." He says, walking behind me.

I keep eye contact with him as I turn the shower on and undress. "Go check on our son." I teasingly waved him out of the bathroom. "And please come home on time tonight so we can celebrate," I yell, stepping into the hot shower. Jamie has a habit of working late. I know he is working hard to ensure the business continues to grow. But sometimes I wish he didn't "lose track of time," as he says he does.

Charly & Jamie 2005

On January 12, 2005, Cari Carol Walsh joined our family. The name Cari comes from the shortened Spanish version of Charlene, Carlota. I'd always loved it when my teachers called me Carlota in Spanish class in high school. Carol is in honor of my aunt and Marie's mom, both of whom lost their battles with breast cancer. It's also special because Cari will share the same initials as me.

I don't plan to return to work since our business continues to succeed, allowing me to stay home. We both have stepped away from the field in which we received our degrees. The construction company was only supposed to get him out of sales. At the same time, he got the hang of flipping houses, and it became a big thing. There are now TV shows about house flipping. He got into the business at just the right time. I'm ecstatic about being home all day with the kids and being there when Jamie gets home from work. It may sound like a scene from a black-and-white Nick at Night television show, but I love Jamie so much and want to ensure we have the best home life possible. I've been trying to become a better cook!

I feel much more relaxed and comfortable with having a newborn now. Cari is an easy baby, and JJ is gentle and sweet with her. Together, they make my role as a mom easier. I enrolled JJ in a preschool closer to our home, which gives me a few hours each day alone with Cari. I've realized that a second child often misses that one-on-one time with a parent. It also helps JJ meet kids with whom he will attend elementary, middle, and high school. I do not worry about meeting or making mom friends. Having lived in Danvers my whole life, I know many of the mothers I run into are people I knew growing up.

Jamie is such a compassionate father. I'm incredibly amazed at how he interacts with Cari. He dotes on her. I catch him whispering, almost baby-talk-like, to her when he is alone, holding her. He is so careful of her, as if he might break her.

"You are Daddy's princess. I am never going to let anyone touch you. No dating until you are 30," I hear Jame saying to her. Jamie is rougher with JJ, as if he is trying to toughen him up for the football field. There's something special in Jamie's eyes when he's with Cari. She will be a daddy's girl for sure.

Something I did not consider when I decided to stop working was the money, or, rather, the lack of my involvement in it. Jamie now manages all of our finances. I trust him implicitly, but a nagging sense of insecurity lingers. It isn't about distrust but about feeling... irrelevant, like a decorative ornament in our financial ecosystem. My mother has influenced me in many ways, the biggest being how she instilled in me the importance of financial independence. This reliance on Jamie, while comfortable in some ways, feels strangely alien to me.

"Jamie," I approached him as he was getting ready for work, "can we have a stay-at-home date on Saturday?"

He grins, a mischievous glint in his eye. "Sure, what do you have in mind?"

"We can do that," I say, "but first, I need to talk to you about something important."

He turns, his brow furrowed. "What's up?"

"Our finances," I explain. "I know you handle everything, and I truly appreciate it. But I feel... detached. I don't know our budget, our savings, or our investments. It makes me feel helpless."

"Helpless?" he echoes, his voice sharp. "Why would you feel helpless? I'm taking care of everything."

"I know," I say gently, "and I trust you completely. But I want to understand. I want to feel involved. It's important to me."

"I provide for you, for this house, for everything! Do you want this lifestyle? Do you want these things?"

His words sting. "Of course I do," I retort. "But I also want to feel like a partner in this, not a... a dependent."

"A dependent?" he scoffs. "Charly, you're not a dependent!" he says with escalating annoyance. "I have built a company. I'm working my ass off to give you and the kids the best life possible! I make sure your account has plenty of money in it so you can go spend it on whatever it is you do all day."

His words cut through me, and tears prick my eyes. "I understand that," I whisper, my voice trembling. "But I need to feel like I'm part of it, not just a beneficiary."

The argument is escalating, fueled by frustration and hurt.

"I don't want to argue, and I don't do whatever all day. I am taking care of our children." I walk away, annoyed and wounded. I hold Cari close, her soft warmth comforting against the icy silence that had descended upon our home.

That night, Jamie is home at 5:30 p.m., which is early for him. We had not talked all day. Our normal check-in throughout the day did not happen, so I am surprised when he pulls into the driveway. I watch him walk in the back door, holding flowers. I can't help smiling as he walks up to me in the kitchen. Handing me the flowers, he looks into my eyes and kisses me.

"I am sorry about this morning. You are right, you should know everything. I got mad because I don't and would never consider you a dependent. You are my partner. You are one of the smartest people in my life. That is one of the reasons I was so attracted to you when we first met. You are so intelligent. I could never think of you as anything less than my partner." I take the flowers and place them on the counter.

"Thank you," I say as I eye the flowers. "And thank you for saying that. It means a lot to me. It also means a lot that you came home early. I know you are working so hard for our family. I appreciate you and your motivation for us. I love the fuck out of you, Jamie Walsh," I whisper in his ear as I hug him.

Saturday night, my mom and dad come over to watch the kids. Jamie and I go out and discuss things over dinner. Just in case things get heated, neither of us would fight in public. Over dinner, Jamie goes over all the finances and shows me where the accounts are and how to access them. We decided that I would pay the utility bills, other small bills, and the kids' preschool fees. We also decide to set up a savings account to use for future family vacations. Jamie is also committed to coming home every day at 5:30 pm and spending time with us. Even if it means later in the night, he does some work.

Charly 2005

Living and working in Boston, I don't find myself going out into the suburbs shopping at malls like I used to. Growing up in the 1980s, I was a "mall rat," as they would say. Up until my early twenties, I worked in different stores and restaurants in the Liberty Tree and North Shore Malls. Back then, I was famously known in the area for working at Chess King, a popular men's clothing store from the 1980s. I have always found comfort in going to one. Something about walking around, going in and out of stores, brings me back to being a teenager when life was carefree and all about having fun.

Driving from my parents' house back to my apartment in the North End, where I moved to. I am finally living on my own in a run-down studio. I decided to stop at the Square One Mall in Saugus. I figure, why not take the opportunity to walk through a mall?

The hum of the mall, a symphony of forgotten desires, washes over me. Abercrombie & Fitch, a cacophony of manufactured cool, assaults my senses. They always play music so loudly. Walking by Hollister, the air thick with cloying sweetness chokes me, a bitter reminder of a youth I no longer recognize.

I make my way to the food court, looking at the options and hoping for a Sabarro, my go-to food court food. I worked at the one in Liberty Tree Mall my first year in high school. For a chain, I still enjoy the pizza. Then, I see him, Jamie Walsh. Walking toward me, a mirage shimmering in the fluorescent light, his smile was a fleeting glimpse of a past I thought I'd buried deep within. My breath speeds up, and I am shaking all over. I did not feel like this when I ran into Peter. There is something different with Jamie, and there always has been. Perhaps Peter felt that, too. I know I played a part in our breakup. I've always struggled with confronting conflict. I am still petrified to be vulnerable. I shut down and would rather walk away from a relationship than be vulnerable and deal with a conflict. I did it with Jamie, then Peter, and if I am honest, Colin.

"Charly, how are you?" I hear my name coming from Jamie as we meet in the middle of the food court.

"Jamie Walsh, what a nice surprise running into you," I say, excited to see him, feeling the heat pulsate through my body. He is still as handsome as ever. I feel as though I have been pulled back in time. I want to give him a big hug and be in his arms again. I wish I had told him how I felt for him years ago instead of running away.

"Yeah, I was picking up something from Brookstone. How has life been treating you?" he says, looking around. He grabs a chair at the table next to him and begins fidgeting with it with his foot.

"It's been good, nothing exciting. I live and work in Boston. How about you?" I ask.

"Good, married, just had our second kid," he shares.

The years melt away as I look at him, revealing the young guy I'd known. I am disappointed to hear he is married, but also happy for him. I wonder who the lucky girl is. Smiling at him, I cannot help but feel that standing here looking at me is uncomfortable for him. His gaze flits nervously around; it seems as though he cannot get out of this conversation fast enough. The weight of unspoken words hangs heavily in the air. The what-ifs claw at my throat. I see the flicker in his eyes, a fleeting echo of the young guy who'd once ignited a fire in my soul.

"I need to get going. I just stopped in here to grab a Diet Coke," Jamie says.

"Well, it was awesome running into you. I'm so happy to hear life is ...going so great for you." I genuinely mean it, although it comes out nervously.

"Same, Charly. It is nice running into you. Take care," Jamie says, walking past me. I turn and watch him walk away. We were so close once, and now I think he cannot stand the sight of me.

Driving home, I can't stop thinking about Jamie, our exchange, and our friendship in school. I miss all of it. I wish things had turned out differently between us. What a strange, serendipitous night.

I met Tony in the North End, the Little Italy neighborhood in Boston, for a cappuccino a few weeks later. Tony got married a year ago in Positano, Italy, and I took the opportunity to attend. Positano and the Amalfi Coast are beautiful, although I may be biased, but I think Costa del Sol, Spain, is better. It is where I started my trip to Tony's wedding to spend time with Colin. I can't be over in Europe and not see him. Spain feels like coming home. I step off the plane and bam, right back into my old life with Colin. I put my things in the closet and place my toothbrush in its usual spot. We fall asleep next to each other and wake up like nothing ever happened, like the breakup was just a bad dream. God, it's exhausting. Emotionally draining. But I can't shake this connection with Colin. And I don't think he can either.

Smiling at Tony, I share my uneasy exchange with Jamie at the mall.

"Maybe you caught him at a bad time. "Tony shares his thoughts. "Not everyone is as excited to see people from their past like you are."

"True, it's sad to me, because he and I were so close at one time." I take a sip of my cappuccino. "I wish I had not ended things the way I did with him. I wish things had turned out differently." I surprise myself by saying the words out loud. I take a few more sips of my cappuccino, watching Tony sip his espresso. He looks so European as he sips. He is wearing a fitted black T-shirt, jeans that fit in the right area and loose in others, a black belt, and black loafers. But it is the way he picks up the tiny mug and sips. I look down at myself, and I am wearing the typical cute top, jeans, and flats, looking all American.

"I've been thinking." I break the silence between us, causing Tony's eyebrows to furrow in question. "I don't want to have children. What do you think about that?"

He places the small ceramic espresso mug down on its saucer and then sits upright in his chair, leaning forward, almost as if he is about to tell me a secret.

"What made you come to that conclusion? You've talked about wanting children before. I remember when you were with Colin, you wanted to have one with him," Tony reminds me. I look into my cappuccino, and the foam has settled into the espresso, making it look like a regular coffee.

"What changed your mind? I hope this doesn't have to do with you two breaking up." Tony asks.

"No, it has nothing to do with Colin. I'm not really sure. I've been watching my friends with their children and seeing how their relationships with their husbands change after having kids. I also think about how I can't even get a guy to want to go on more than a few dates with me, let alone find someone who wants to have children with me someday." I laugh a bit, realizing the comment about men seems irrelevant. "But seriously, it just hit me one day that having a child is not some-

thing I envision in my life." Or maybe the back and forth with Colin is confusing me more than I realize. He's been vocal about not wanting children. No, I know being truthful with myself, it doesn't have to do with Colin.

"I think once you meet the right person, you might change your mind, especially if that person wants kids," Tony advises.

"Or I could find a man who doesn't want children either?" I challenge him.

"You're young and have plenty of time. I think you'll change your mind eventually," Tony says.

"I don't think I will. This feels right for me, it's a decision from my soul," I tell him.

I lean back and glance around the café. A few older men are sitting at a table speaking Italian, as a group of tourists enters and sits at a table next to us. Being in the North End feels like being in Italy.

"I think I'm going to get a pastry. Do you want anything?" I ask Tony.

"I'm good," he replies.

I get up and walk to the counter to order my pastry. I glance back at Tony; we have been friends since 1989, and our friendship has become more meaningful and supportive as we've grown older. I smile at him as he looks my way and smiles back. Friendships are easy, not complicated like the relationships I have had with men. Romantic relationships are complex, challenging, and an obligation; that may be my problem. I know my problem; I don't feel safe being vulnerable with a guy, or maybe I just haven't been with the right guy.

Charly & Jamie 2007

My routine as a stay-at-home mom has become predictable. I get up early with the kids. Sometimes, we hang out in the bedroom, watching Jamie get ready for work. We have some family conversations, or the kids run around while I try to talk a little with Jamie while he gets ready for work.

This morning, I decided to take the kids downstairs to start our day. Standing at the kitchen island, sipping my coffee, I watch the kids eat their breakfast. JJ is having dry cereal because he doesn't like milk in it, while Cari enjoys her cereal with milk and is getting better at feeding herself with a spoon.

Lately, a nagging unease has settled over me. Though I relish the freedom of staying home with JJ and Cari, a quiet discontent simmers beneath the surface. I'd thought staying home would be different. But instead, I yearn for a sense of purpose, a contribution beyond motherhood.

"What are you guys doing today?" Jamie asks as he comes into the kitchen. He grabs a mug and pours himself some coffee. He walks over to me, slides his hand onto the small of my back, and kisses me on the cheek. He kisses each of the kids and then sits down to sip his coffee. Jamie is back on track with spending time in the morning with us by sitting at the table for at least 15 minutes before he leaves for the office. I join them at the table, cupping Cari's head in my hand while she tilts her head and looks up at me, and I smile at her.

"We're going to Aunt Marie's," I say excitedly to get the kids pumped up. "JJ and Cari get to play with Jack and Kimmie." The best part is that Marie and I have kids close in age. Marie and I take turns at whose house we playdate a couple of times a week, so the kids can play together. Jamie and I send the kids to daycare and preschool for three hours a day during the school year, but we don't send them during the summer to save money.

"Well, I'm jealous! I want to play with you guys, Jack, and Kimmie," Jamie says to JJ and Cari.

"Come play with us, Daddy!" JJ shouts.

"Actually, Marie and Matt invited all of us over for a barbecue on Sunday. Daddy can play with you all then," I tell them, and they cheer excitedly. I glance at Jamie to see if he's okay with going.

"Whatever you want," he says, and shrugs with a smile. That kind of answer always rubs me the wrong way. Part of me wants to ask outright if he even wants to go. But honestly, I'm just so tired of being the sole planner for our family. Somewhere along the way, I've become a wife, mom, and full-time entertainment director. I'm losing touch with my own interests, constantly focused on figuring out everyone else's. That's why when Marie and Matt suggest hanging out, I jump at the chance.

"I can pick up steak tips at Danvers Butchery," I say, hoping that will make him happier about going.

"Teriyaki, please," Jamie requests.

"Is there really any other kind?" I respond sarcastically but honestly.

"I don't like leaving my beautiful, amazing family. It breaks my heart, but Daddy has to go to work," Jamie says as he gets up, putting his mug in the sink. I take a deep breath, watching him. He could put it in the dishwasher, but instead leaves it for me to do.

"No!" JJ shouts to Jamie.

"I'll rush home," Jamie says, pointing at the clock on the wall. "When the big hand is on the six, and the little hand is on the 5, I'll be home," he explains to the kids. They're too young to understand fully, but I think it's cute how Jamie tries to make everything educational. I stand and walk to the door with Jamie.

"Have fun with Marie," Jamie tells me. I try not to feel guilty that I get to spend the day with my best friend while he works. It is not a life I thought I would ever live. I also have a persistent guilt about my parents' investment in an education that now feels unused. It's easy to forget that I even possess a Bachelor's degree, the years of effort that I seem to have sidelined. My current life path offers little evidence of the years I spent earning my degree. There's a quiet shame in the realization that the hard-won knowledge sits dormant. I cling to the hope that my parents find solace in the family I've created, perhaps overlooking the path not taken.

"I will," I smile at him. He leans in to kiss me and surprises me with a full-on tongue-in-the-mouth kiss. My body heats up, and I feel tingly all over. He still excites me, and the guilt and annoyance wash away, replaced by sexual excitement.

"Your ass is mine tonight after the kids are asleep," he says in a low voice in my ear.

"After that kiss, are you going to make me wait all day?" I pout to him.

"Be ready, I love the fuck out of you," he whispers, eyeing the kids to make sure they do not hear him swear.

Later that afternoon, Marie helps me bring the kids to the car. Cari had fallen asleep, so I carried her while she walked with JJ.

Once I get the kids buckled in, I hug and thank Marie. I look behind her and see Jack and Kimmie standing on the back steps.

"Thank you guys, I love you," I say to them and wave.

"Bye, Auntie Cha Cha," they yell back to me. I get in the car and watch Marie and the kids go back in the house. Marie is a fantastic mother. Everything she does is for the sake of her kids. It may not make sense to them or Matt, but I know it is always for the best of the kids. She makes me strive to be a better mom.

A wave of melancholy washes over me as I pull out of the driveway. I love my children fiercely, Jamie deeply. But a part of me, a long-dormant part, yearns for something more. What if I had never met Jamie, or we ended up not getting together and going our separate ways? The truth is, a part of me secretly yearns for the woman I might have become.

I hear the familiar sounds of a train and the ringing of bells as the crossing gates come down over the road—the commuter rail.

"JJ, look out the window next to Cari. A train is coming," I tell him as he leans forward to look out the window. I smile while watching him; he is so sweet. I hope I am raising him to be a good person.

As the train rumbles past and stops, a group of commuters emerges. Men in suits, laptop bags over their shoulders, women in stylish dresses and sneakers juggling purses and other bags. These are the women I thought I would be, the ones who navigate the city, pursue their passions, and build careers. The image of myself as a career woman, independent and ambitious, feels both foreign and strangely alluring. I would be Charly Carlen, not Mrs. Walsh, not just a mother and a wife. A reminder of a path not taken, the person I might have become.

"Do you think you and David will have kids?" I ask Melissa, watching JJ and Cari squeal delightfully on their swing set. Her wedding to David, who had been a cook at Supino's when we worked there in our twenties, is just months away. Since leaving Marie's, I'd found myself grappling with the what-ifs—what if I had pursued my career in Boston, climbing the corporate ladder at some prestigious fitness center? What if Jamie and I had delayed parenthood, savoring our freedom a little longer, perhaps waiting until our mid-thirties?

"We have talked about it," Melissa replies. "I think we will, eventually."

"Is it... wrong?" I say, "to sometimes wonder what my life would be like without them?"

Melissa's eyes fill with warmth. "You are an incredible mom, Charly. I can't imagine you any other way. I knew you would be an amazing mother from the moment I met you."

Her words are a balm to my soul, yet a nagging doubt remains. "I feel guilty even thinking such things," I admit. "Honestly, I don't think I would have had children without Jamie."

"Oh, you would have," Melissa assures me. "With someone else, perhaps. You would also have different children."

I ponder her words, gazing at my children as they play. Their laughter, their innocent joy, fills the air with a warmth that I can't imagine living without. I look around the yard, the vibrant flower beds, the lush green lawn, a testament to Jamie's green thumb (a talent I sorely lack).

This life, with all its messy beauty, is mine. It is a life filled with love, laughter, and occasional chaos. As I return to the patio with a fresh bottle of wine, I realize that maybe, just maybe, this unexpected path is the one I am meant to walk.

The following week, I join my "Danvers girls" for our once-a-quarter dinner, a tradition we've upheld for a few years, especially since so many of us have started families. All but two of us now navigate the joys and challenges of motherhood. Jen N., or rather, Jen W. now, is still buzzing from the arrival of her third child, her exhaustion palpable yet outweighed by the radiant glow of new motherhood. She's organized the gathering, a much-needed escape from the chaos of her household.

I cherish these dinners, a sanctuary of shared experiences. Having grown up together, we know each other inside and out. When we get together, the laughter flows freely, seasoned with sarcasm, banter, and teasing. We commiserate over sleepless nights, the tyranny of tantrums, and the occasional exasperating quirks of our husbands. It is all good-natured complaining, a tacit acknowledgment of the shared burdens and the enduring bonds of motherhood.

"CC, did you see Michael Dowd opened a dental office in Danvers?" Jen W. asks me. Michael, or Mikey as I called him, was my boyfriend throughout high school. For some reason, my friends think I care about what he does. I do not, and I don't even think about him.

"Good for him. I have a dentist I am very happy with, I will not be changing," I tell the table.

"He would probably pull all your teeth out," jokes Marie.

"He couldn't care less about me, the same way I don't care about him," I respond. What I really want to say is, "*Have you seen my hot husband? My nice, compassionate, intelligent, and successful husband? Why would I even think about Mikey?*" But I don't. I am always very cautious not to boast about how lucky I am that I have Jamie. Plus, the last time I saw Mikey was at our high school graduation. Mikey made it known that he can't stand me for some reason. He has never spoken to me since we broke up at the beginning of senior year. He would ignore me when he had to be near me after we broke up.

As we are all hugging and saying goodbye in the foyer, a guy we went to high school with walks in.

"Hi Scott, nice to see you," I say. Some of the other girls say hi as well.

"Hi, wow, you all look exactly the same," he says. "I can't believe you're still friends?"

"Yeah, why wouldn't we be?" I ask.

"I don't know. It is rare for a group of high school friends to remain so close this long after," he says.

"I could not imagine why we wouldn't still be friends," I tell him.

"Yeah, same," a few of the other girls say.

"You guys are lucky to have each other," he says to us, "great seeing you."

I smile at my friends. We *are* lucky, and I hope our friendships stay this way for the rest of our lives.

Charly 2010

I would say that 2010 is one of the longest years of my life. After a two-year relationship and living together, I went through another breakup. The kicker with this one is that I moved into his apartment in South Boston, or "Southie" as locals call it, leaving my place in the North End. I had loved living in my own run-down studio apartment.

Thankfully, I didn't play a part in this breakup. He cheated on me and confessed to doing so. Saying it was a drunken mistake, that he wanted to be with me. I tried for nine months to see if I could get over it. I couldn't, so here I am.

Although I would love to return to the North End, I can't afford it on my own anymore. The cost of rent has skyrocketed across the city. I answered a roommate ad on Craigslist. The girl looking wins me over when I tell her I am moving out from living with my now ex-boyfriend.

"We all hurt from breakups. You are going to be okay," she tells me during our meeting. "It takes a while, but you get a fresh start, especially if you want to move in with me."

The apartment ends up being only half a mile from the one I had been living in with my ex. But the half a mile feels like living in a different neighborhood. I take a different bus to and from work. I use a different laundromat and different corner stores to pick up items *from. I am also closer to my gym and the grocery store. I have come to appreciate the area and my new surroundings. Bonnie, my new room-mate, is the same age, and she's an incredibly generous person and hysterical. I settle into my single life, having a roommate again and knowing that I can handle what life throws at me.*

I look out the window of the commuter rail train as I head to the an-nual Yankee swap with the Danvers girls. We annually partake in the New England Christmas tradition of exchanging gifts. Where every-one picks a number, and then we go around picking from the gifts we each brought in numerical order. The rules, although I have never seen official rules, always seem to be a bit different depending on the group of people. With us, the rules seem to change each year, depending on everyone's mood. Michelle is picking me up at Beverly Depot, and then we will drive to Brittany's house in Amesbury. People often tell us it's rare for a group like ours to remain friends, but I don't understand why. Why would we stop being friends because we're no longer in high school? I have many other friends, but with the Danvers girls, there's a unique bond.

As I gaze out the window, I watch the scenery. I've ridden this train many times and never get tired of it. I pass the triple-deckers in Chelsea, the Revere marshes, and the shopping plazas in Lynn. I see fa-miliar roads that I've driven countless times. In Swampscott, I think about the family I babysat for and my friend Nessa. When the train passes through Salem, I can spot Roslyn Street where two girlfriends live. The North Shore, I can't imagine growing up anywhere else. I love that this is my home.

"Next stop, Beverly Depot," the conductor announces. As the train begins to slow down, I look for Michelle's car as the train pulls into the

depot. I spot her sitting in her car on the other side of the tracks. I wave and walk over to her.

"Hey, what's up?" I ask, settling into the passenger seat.

"Hey, lady, how are you doing?" Michelle replies.

"All is good with me," I tell her.

Michelle drives off and heads toward Amesbury. She talks most of the way about her work as a hygienist and complains about one of her sisters. Michelle tells me about a guy she's seeing; she always has a funny story about him.

"Hello!" Michelle and I say in unison as we walk through Brittany's front door.

"In here!" someone yells from the kitchen.

Brittany beautifully decorated her house for Christmas, wrapping the stair railing in greenery and adorning a Christmas tree with fairy lights that reach the second-floor landing. In the kitchen, I see Jen W. and Marie coming in from the living room.

"Everyone needs to pick a number out of the bowl," Brittany announces as she walks around with it.

"How are we playing this year? Can we only take the gift before us?" I ask, knowing this topic often leads to debate. Every year, we go through this with rules; I swear, we change them every year.

"No, we can pick any available gift," Michelle interjects.

"I don't like that," I reply, but my argument doesn't win, and the gift exchange goes smoothly this year.

Standing at the kitchen island, I can't stop eating the meatballs. "Who brought the meatballs?" I ask, reaching for another and peeking into the crock-pot to ensure some are still there. Even though we always have way too much food, someone will notice I ate them all. I glance around the room, seeing Michelle and Jen W. huddled on the couch, talking and laughing.

"Remember that time we drove around..." I hear Michelle say, not hearing what Jen W. said before they both explode into laughter. Marie, side-eyeing them as she walked by towards me. Marie, thankfully, had recently moved back with her family from Houston.

"Oh boy, what are they up to now? You know when they get like that, something is going to happen." Marie stops next to me.

"Who knows with those two?" I mumble while eating another meatball.

"I am going to get another glass of wine, you good?" Marie asks, holding up her glass.

I look down at my half-glass of wine. "I'm good". I look up as I see Jen W. and Michelle coming towards me.

"In coming," Marie says as she walks off.

"Charly, we have to tell you something," Michelle says, laughing with Jen W. on the opposite side of the island.

"What?" I ask, curious.

"One time, we stuffed a condom with sausages and left it on your parents' steps," Michelle reveals.

"It was her idea," Jen W. adds, pointing at Michelle.

I watch them laughing, trying to figure out what the heck they are talking and laughing about. I have no idea what.... Then it hits me: it wasn't Jamie who'd left the condom stuffed with sausages on my parents' steps, it was them!

"That was you guys?! What the fuck. I thought this guy I was friends with and hooking up with did it. I stopped talking to him because of that. Ugh! Why did you guys do that?" I sigh.

Michelle and Jen W. laugh harder. Jen W. squeezes out "I'm sorry" through her laughter. I start laughing at the absurdity of it all.

"Who knows why we did it? I think we were driving around town and decided to do it," Michelle explains. "I am sure we thought it would be funny for you to find it in the morning."

I can't believe it was them and not Jamie, I think, then wince, thinking about my awkward encounter with Jamie years ago at the Square One mall. Remember how I had abruptly cut him off from my life. It handled that badly; no wonder he could not get away from me fast enough.

Charly 2013

I can hardly believe that I am turning 40 on March 29th. The years have flown by; it is strange how, as you get older, the years seem to go faster. I finally feel like I have a career rather than just a job. Becoming an addiction counselor has been the best decision I could have made. It always sounds weird when I tell people why I decided to become one, because you only hear nuns or priests say this. But I got a calling. I was out for a run, and I heard as clear as day that I should become a substance abuse counselor. It is the height of the opioid epidemic in Massachusetts. I was miserable working an administrative job from one corporate office to another. I enrolled in a certificate program at the University of Massachusetts Boston. Going back to classes on campus was a trip. It brought back many memories of my time there during my undergraduate studies. Especially Jamie; there were no cute guys like him this time. Once I completed the program, passed the state exam, and began working in the field, I realized that this is my true purpose in life. It comes naturally to me, and I excel at it. I wake up every day looking forward to going to work.

I work at a homeless shelter in the middle of downtown Boston. All walks of life come in and out of the doors all day. As much as I plan for the day, something can change it in an instant. A crisis can arise from my walking up on individuals in the stairwell using substances, and *me needing to call security over the walkie-talkie. Or I have a client I am helping reconnect with family, who has not spoken to them in a decade due to his addiction. My colleagues are fun, supportive team players. We are exposed to a lot, and some days, a few of us need to sit in the lunchroom and talk about a mindless television show as self-care.*

Reflecting on my journey, I wish I had gotten married by now. I have been in and out of relationships and been on what felt like a million dates. With any man I have dated, Colin is always at the back of my mind, hoping he would change his mind and ask me to marry him. We continue to fall back into our old dynamics on my yearly trips to Spain for vacations.

My decision not to have children at a young age was the right one for me. I am still extremely happy with that choice. If I had chosen to have children, I don't think I would have pursued this career. I believe that my intuition guided me so that I would be able to step into this work. I wouldn't have gained the life experiences necessary to understand myself and provide guidance to my clients. However, having a husband is something I truly desire in my life now. As I get older, I fear that it might never happen. I try to stay hopeful and hope that each new man I get involved with will be the one. My plans for my 40th are to go to Spain. If I am honest, I am hoping that this will be the year that Colin finally says, "let's be together". But if he doesn't. I will come home to my friends, and I feel incredibly fortunate to have them. My friendships have given me more love than I could have ever imagined. They are my chosen family, built on shared history, inside jokes, mutual respect, and a deep understanding of each other's journey. My friendships truly nourish my soul.

Charly & Jamie 2015

Christmas has never really been a holiday I've enjoyed. I have always felt as though there is so much build-up and pressure to be perfect. I rely on Jamie to weave the magic for the children, to transform our home into a winter wonderland. But Christmas Eve... now that's a different story. Christmas Eve holds a special place in my heart, a cherished echo of childhood.

Back then, my grandmother Carlen hosted an open house on Christmas Eve. Family, friends, and neighbors all came to my grandparents' house. A month before, when the Sears and Roebuck catalog arrived, a wave of excitement would wash over me. My mother would let me choose any dress I desired, and I'd spend hours poring over the pages, imagining myself twirling and laughing amidst the festive crowd.

I still have pictures of myself, a vision in head-to-toe velour, those dresses adorned with an abundance of lace ruffles. Looking back, I can almost feel the softness of the fabric against my skin, the thrill of anticipation in the air. Those Christmas Eves, filled with the warmth of family and the magic of childhood, are a cherished part of who I am.

As my grandparents got older, I took over the tradition so they could relax while I hosted. My parents, brother Travis, uncles, aunts, and cousins would drop in. Jamie's mother, aunts, uncles, and cousins would come. We had friends who would stop by. It was fun and festive, and the best night of the holiday season for me. The kids always got to open one gift that night. They used to eye the gifts for days leading up to Christmas Eve, deciding which gift to open.

Now, the holidays have taken on a frenetic pace. The kids, with their jam-packed schedules, are pulled in a hundred different directions. Basketball games, holiday concerts, and school parties seem to encroach on every waking moment. Ever the dedicated coach, Jamie spends countless hours on the sidelines, cheering on JJ's basketball team while juggling Cari's volleyball practice schedule. I've also become the unofficial party hostess for the kids and their friends and teammates, hosting countless end-of-season bashes and holiday gatherings for them. I revel in the process, using Pinterest and other social media platforms to find decorating inspirations.

Jamie's company holiday party is another event I try to navigate with a delicate touch. I leave the logistical details to his capable office administrators, striving to maintain a healthy distance from his professional life. I've witnessed the pitfalls of the "owner's wife" trope, and I'm determined to avoid that fate. I want to be a supportive partner, not a looming presence.

The familiar rhythm of Christmas at home is about to break this year. We are so busy all year that we need time to stop and enjoy each other as a family. I've broached the idea of a Christmas vacation with Jamie to somewhere warm, a tropical escape while it is cold and miserable here. To my surprise, Jamie is for it. The kids, surprisingly, are ecstatic. I make the promise to have Christmas Eve still, as long as everyone promises to help clean up after, so we can leave for our trip in the morning.

"You're leaving us on Christmas?" My mother's voice is a mixture of disbelief and concern.

"Mom," I explain patiently, "we haven't spent every Christmas together for years. You and Dad alternate between our house and Clay's."

"It's not the same," she insists, her voice tinged with a familiar brand of maternal worry. "Knowing you won't be in the country..."

"You'll be fine, Mom," I assure her, "you won't even notice we're gone."

"Yes, I will," she counters, "I won't be able to talk to you all."

"I'll call you before we leave for the airport," I promise. "Our flight isn't until 2 p.m."

With a final hug and a flurry of well-wishes, my parents depart. Closing the door, I exhale, surveying the remnants of the evening's festivities. Jamie and Cari are already tidying up.

"JJ, please come help us clean," I call out.

"Coming!" he yells back, his footsteps echoing down the hall.

"Thank you," I say, relieved. "Are you all packed and ready to go?"

"Yes, Mom, just need to get ready in the morning," Cari replies.

"I still have to pack," JJ admits.

"JJ!" Jamie's voice booms. "Pack tonight. We don't want to be rushing around tomorrow morning."

"Okay, okay," JJ grumbles, finally succumbing to the inevitable.

As I settle into bed, Jamie joins me. "He's packing," he confirms, a hint of amusement in his voice.

"Thank you," I say, grateful for his assistance. "How are you feeling about this getaway?"

"Honestly, I can't wait," he says. "I've told everyone at work that unless someone is dead, I'm not answering calls or emails. I even turned off all notifications. I'm... tired, Charly. Not tired in the need-to-sleep sense, but tired from work. Burnt out, I think."

"I had no idea you were feeling this way," I say, sitting up to face him.

"When you suggested this, it felt like a lifeline. I don't know how you knew, but you always have this uncanny intuition."

"I just felt like it was something we needed as a family," I explain.

"That's what makes you amazing," he says, his eyes twinkling. Reminding me that was the exact look in his eyes the day we bumped into each other at the Kiss 108 concert. "You know what we need before we even know it ourselves."

"Thank you," I reply, feeling a warmth spread through me. We fall into a comfortable silence, the anticipation of our vacation a pleasant hum beneath the surface.

"Hey," I say, breaking the silence, "I think it's time I go back to work."

"You don't have to," he says quickly, "we're fine financially."

"I know, but it's something I've been thinking about a lot. I once dreamed of a fulfilling career. I don't feel purposeful and... well, now I'm just... here."

"My feelings for you haven't changed," he assures me, "whether you work or not."

"I know, but it's something I want for myself," I insist. "I remember wishing I'd double-majored in college, maybe in psychology. I realized how much I enjoyed the psychological aspects of fitness while I was working."

"You want to be a psychiatrist?" he asks.

"No, a therapist, a counselor," I explain.

"A guidance counselor?" he asks.

"No, like a therapist someone goes to talk about their problems," I explain.

"Have you looked into any programs?" he says.

"No, not yet. But I will when we get back," I say, a new-found excitement bubbling within me.

"If it's something you truly want, I'm all for it," he says, his voice filled with encouragement. "You'd make an amazing therapist."

"You really think so?" I ask, a smile playing on my lips.

"Absolutely. You're an incredible listener, always honest and insightful." He pulls me close, his embrace warm and reassuring. "Now, let's get some sleep. We have a big day tomorrow."

As I drift off to sleep, the prospect of a new chapter, both in my personal and professional life, fills me with a sense of hope and excitement. This Christmas, I realize, would be a turning point, a time for renewal and rediscovery.

Charly 2016

My love life shifts when Mark enters my life. Before him, I had been holding on to Colin. But when I met Mark, I knew it was time to let go of Colin. It was time to put all of me into one person. Colin had been making empty promises to me. I was growing tired of them.

From the first time I saw Mark, I had been drawn to his magnetic energy. After work one day, I went into The Shannon Tavern, a dive bar that's become my hangout place in Southie. I am one of the regulars there now. Old Steve, not to be confused with Hot Steve, was sitting at the bar. A few other people I didn't know were sitting at the bar as well. I said hi to Old Steve and asked if he minded if I sat on the stool beside him. He said no, so I sat down. The owner and bartender, Jerry, came over to take my drink order. I started chatting with Steve, who was being grumpy. As I took a sip of my beer, I heard a guy a few stools down say, "Wow, Steve, not only is this beautiful woman admitting that she knows you, but she's also willing to sit next to you, and you can't even have a conversation with her."

Steve and I laughed. I turned to look at the guy who had just complimented me and teased Steve. He looked like he had just stepped off a boat from "Wicked Tuna." His head was shaved bald, and he had a goatee that would make him look like Santa Claus if grown to a full beard. He was wearing a black hoodie, jeans, and work boots. Today was the first time I had seen him here, despite having visited for three years. He wasn't conventionally handsome in a way that turned heads, but there was something manly about him. Before I could say anything to him, he put some cash on the bar and said, "See ya, Jerry. See ya, Steve," and walked out.

A few weeks later, I went into The Shannon. Hot Steve was sitting at the bar talking to the guy from a few weeks ago. Hot Steve and I had developed a friendship from hanging out at the bar. He is a handsome, sweet guy. He is my brother's age, 13 years younger than me, and as much as people tried to get me to forget my age and make a move on Hot Steve, I couldn't. I think it was the combination of knowing he was my brother's age, and I did not want to ruin our friendship. Settling into the stool next to Steve, we start catching up. I look at the guy sitting on the other side of Steve and make eye contact. I reach my hand across Steve to the guy and introduce myself.

"You two don't know each other?" Steve says, looking back and forth between the guy and me. "You two are my best friends here. How have you two never met? I hang out with both of you all the time."

"I am Mark," he tells me as he shakes my hand.

"Nice to meet you. "I say to Mark. We realize Mark typically leaves the bar in the afternoons by the time I get out of work and go in. Mark's relationship just ended, so he did not leave the bar as early as he used to. I start seeing Mark more often. Each time I see him, I grow more and more attracted to him. I learn he is a lobsterman. He goes out at 4 a.m. on a lobster boat, lays traps, and catches lobsters. The boats are back on the dock by 3 p.m. There is a dock in South Boston that I had no idea existed. I go down a few times with Mark. It is like another world—it feels like I am in Gloucester, MA, rather than South Boston.

Mark and I do a slow build of our relationship. After two months of dates and some sleepovers, we became boyfriend and girlfriend. Mark and I ride a rollercoaster of our relationship for the next two *years. Mark suffers from severe depression and uses alcohol to mask it. Mark disappears on me sometimes, and I won't hear from him for days. He says he is locked in his apartment the whole time. Our relationship in the good times is magical.*

Mark decides to come to Spain with me to visit Sasha for her 40th birthday. Our week in Spain brings us closer than we have ever been. We can't keep our hands off each other. We make love as much as possible everywhere we can in the timeshare we are staying in.

Mark is a lot more adventurous than I am. He does things just on the edge of breaking the rules.

We spend much of our relationship socializing at The Shannon Tavern or hanging out at my apartment. Mark is great at lying in bed, reading, or cuddling on the couch while watching a TV series. He has me hooked on Vikings and Pinkie Masters. Cuddling on the couch and binge-watching a show is my favorite time with Mark. We often end up making love on the couch. Sex with Mark is slow and sensual. He always starts gently and builds his passion with me.

Mark becomes another man who proves difficult to be in a relationship with. Mark has his issues and struggles, which prevent him from being emotionally available to me. I don't have stability in Mark. I talk to him about it repeatedly, but he has issues he can't work through. It leaves me again loving a man I can't have. I want a partner, a man I can depend on, who shows up for me.

Then, on Sunday, May 8, 2016, life with Mark comes crashing down on me in a way no one could have expected. Leaving a Reiki appointment in the Back Bay, I notice a couple of missed calls from Hot Steve. I feel nausea in the pit of my stomach—he never calls me. I see he left a voicemail as well.

"Charly, it's Steve. Please give me a call back when you get this."

Stepping outside the building, I breathe in the fresh air and call Steve back.

"*Charly,*" *Steve says on the second ring.*

"*Hey, what's up?*" *I ask.*

"*It's Mark,*" *Steve says.*

"*What happened?*" *I ask. The first thing that comes to mind is that he went out on a boat this morning and was involved in an accident.*

"*Mark shot himself....*" *Steve barely says the words in his cracked voice.*

"*What, he doesn't have a gun,*" *I say to Steve as I look around. People are walking along the sidewalk and living their everyday lives. Meanwhile, I think I may throw up, and my legs are weak.*

"*Yes, he did, Charly. He had an old one. Skip found him in his bed.*" *Steve tells me. Skip is Mark's roommate.*

"*Is he at a hospital?*" *I ask.*

"*No. Skip said there is no way he is alive by how he shot himself. Skip called 911, and they pronounced at the scene,*" *Steve explains.*

"*I am in Back Bay, heading back to Southie now,*" *I say. That is all I could say; nothing made sense. None of this made any sense. Why would he do this? He would not do this.*

"*I am sorry, Charly,*" *Steve says.*

"*I am sorry,*" *I say to Steve. I did not know what else to say or do. This can't be true. I will get back to Southie, and Mark will be there, and this will all have been a mistake.*

When I return to the neighborhood, the reality of Mark's death hits me hard. It is not a mistake. I have experienced death in my life before, and honestly, I thought I was strong enough to handle grief. However, nothing can prepare a person for the shock of suicide. I have never felt grief like this before. All I want is for Mark to knock at my door and tell me it was all a mistake. I want people to take away the pain of grief. I want them to understand what I'm going through. Nothing seems to ease the heartache.

Sitting in my apartment, having consumed a bottle of wine and a couple of beers, I realize I don't even feel a buzz. It's 4 p.m., and despite drinking a lot, the alcohol isn't affecting me. Lying here, with no TV on and music playing at a low volume, I wonder if this is the pain that Mark spoke about. I remember once asking him to stop drinking. He told me he had tried, but after about three days, the pain became too unbearable, and the alcohol helped numb it. I could never have imagined the depth of the pain he felt. Now, lying here with this physical ache—heaviness, emptiness, and hurt, nothing seems to relieve it. If I close my eyes and sleep, it fades away. Mark had wanted his pain to go away permanently. That permanence meant leaving his life and all of us behind.

A friend asked if I feel guilty about Mark. I get why. Being a substance abuse counselor, I guess the expectation is that I should have seen it and fixed it. I'd known about the alcohol, yes. But I also know you can't force someone to stop. And the depression, yes, I'd known and at times used our relationship as leverage for him to seek help. But here's the thing I've learned: no matter what you do, what you know, tragedy can still touch you, touch those you love. My profession didn't prevent this, but it did help me understand it. And in that understanding, I find my answer. No. No guilt. No responsibility. I know, deep down, I'd done everything I could. And in that knowing, there's a sense of peace, a step toward healing.

Thank goodness for friends. Many of them rally around me. I don't know what I need, but thankfully, those living nearby know how to help. Gisele, who lives in the building in front of me, brings me breakfast every morning, while Bonnie arrives with bags filled with snacks. Other friends stop by, even when I insist that I'm okay. I realize I have difficulty allowing others to care for me; I often feel that I am undeserving of their kindness.

When I called Melissa about Mark's death, she urged me to come to visit her in Savannah, saying it would be good for me to get away and heal. I took her up on the offer and spent six weeks with her and her family. She cooks me homemade meals every night and brings me to yoga classes during the day, and we take walks in the hot Savannah heat. It is precisely what I need. I fell in love with the city; there is something about it that feels like I belong there.

Charly 2017

The familiar white, with rainbow-colored paint, *gas tank is a beacon on countless road trips on Route 93 and now brings a fresh wave of tears. I am leaving Boston, leaving behind a life, a love, a part of myself. The move to Savannah feels like a leap into the unknown, a desperate attempt to escape the suffocating grief that clings to me like a shroud. Mark's death casts a long shadow; some days are heavy and oppressive, while distant aches mark others. But it is always there, a constant reminder of my love for him.*

With its Spanish moss-draped oaks and sultry Southern humidity, Savannah offers a different kind of rhythm. The anonymity of a new city is both liberating and isolating. No one here knows my story, my heartbreak. No one tilts their head sympathetically, asking the inevitable, "How are you doing?" The initial relief of anonymity quickly gives way to a profound loneliness. I realize I need to be seen, to be heard, to allow myself to be vulnerable. That is what I have been struggling with my whole life: the fear of being vulnerable. There have been a few friends with whom I have let my guard down, allowing them to see me. But most people, especially romantic partners, only see what I am comfortable letting them see.

Determined to rebuild my life, I am pursuing a master's degree in addiction studies. I hold an undergraduate degree in exercise physiol-

ogy and a certificate in substance abuse counseling. My education enables me to adopt a mind-body approach with my clients. Earning the degree is the next step in my career growth. The demands of school, coupled with part-time work, help keep the grief at bay. On what would have been Mark's birthday, I secured a small, charming carriage house in the heart of historic Savannah, which feels like he was making it happen. It is a haven, a place to heal.

Slowly, I begin to put down roots. I discover the joys of exploring the city on foot, stumbling upon hidden courtyards and charming squares. I find solace in my work, helping others navigate their own struggles, a poignant reminder that life, even in the face of immense loss, can still offer meaning and purpose.

The heat in the south can be oppressive at times. Despite it, I enjoy going for walks in my neighborhood. I check out the landscape of homes, smile, and say hello to people walking past me. One late afternoon, as I walked a bit further than I usually do, I discovered a bar. One thing I have learned about myself is that I love a good neighborhood bar. I made amazing relationships in Southie by going into a dive bar, who knows, this could be my new Shannon Tavern. A man, about ten years older than me, is bartending. Two other people are sitting at the bar; they look up at me, then turn back to their conversation.

"What can I get you?" The bartender asks. Smiling, I glance to see what is on tap. "We do two for one on beer and wine from 4 - 6 pm." He informs me. Checking my watch, it is 5:35 pm.

"Oh, I still get the happy hour. Can I get a cider?" I ask.

"You got it." He turns to the taps and pours. As the bartender puts down my drink in front of me, the door swings open. A woman walks in, bringing the wind with her, the blazing sun glowing behind her. She flops herself onto the stool two over from me. She orders a dirty martini and turns to me.

"I don't normally drink something this strong so early in the evening. But I just got off a call with my divorce attorney. You know how that goes, or I hope you don't. Hi, I'm Celeste." She extends her hand.

"I'm Charly, nice to meet you." I can't help but stare at her. Celeste is a stunning, almost angel-looking woman. She is tall, at least 5'10, most definitely 6' in heels. She is thin, with long blonde hair, blue eyes, and dressed as if she stepped out of a page of Vogue. I assume from her entrance into the bar that she is the type of woman who commands a room when she walks in. She slides to the stool next to me.

"Do you come here often? Oh god, don't answer that. I realize how cheesy that sounded as I said it." Celeste laughs, waving her hand in front of her face.

I laugh, "No, this is my first time in here. I live in the neighborhood, was out for a walk, and here I am." I hold up my cider to cheer her. "Sorry about your divorce, "I add.

"Thanks, I was a mess a few months ago, but now I'm just angry." She smiles, holding up her martini. Celeste and I end up sitting there talking for hours, discovering how much we have in common. She went to school in Massachusetts from Minnesota, lived with her boyfriend in Boston, who also sadly passed away, but from a drug overdose. She then moved to Savannah with her now soon-to-be ex-husband. Celeste and I agree to meet the following week at the bar. Our meetings turn into weekly dates and a growing friendship. As she talks about her life after marriage, I'm reminded of how I've rebuilt my life several times. I'm doing it again, and I know I'll be okay. The constant thought in my mind is "everything is working out for me." My life may not look the way I imagined, but here I am, making another friend, adding to the many friends I already have around the world. It seems like everything is working out for me, right?

Charly & Jamie 2019

I've always wanted to go back to Savannah, GA, ever since I visited for St. Patrick's Day spring break in 1993. The name conjures up images of moss-draped oaks and cobblestone streets, a romantic echo of a spring break trip decades ago. Ever the thoughtful planner, Jamie had surprised me with this weekend getaway to celebrate my achievement: becoming a licensed mental health counselor.

Travel has fallen by the wayside in recent years. Early in our marriage, money was tight. Later, it was always about the kids, their schedules, their needs. This trip, just the two of us, feels like a long-overdue exhale. Sitting in the rental car, I realize how much I've missed this: simply being with him, no responsibilities, just the open road and the rhythm of our conversation.

"What are you smiling about?" Jamie asks, his hand resting lightly on my thigh.

"Just appreciating the silence," I admit, "no kids asking questions, no schedules to keep. It's... nice to be Charly again."

"Who is Charly?" he muses, his eyes twinkling.

"Who was I before all of this?" I say more to myself than to him. "Before the kids, before the career... I've spent so much time figuring out everyone else that I've lost sight of myself."

"You've always been sweet, kind, intelligent," he counters, his voice firm. "Beautiful inside and out. And right now," he adds, glancing at me with a look of desire, "You incredibly turn me on."

That night, perched at a rooftop bar overlooking the Savannah River, the city lights shimmering below, we rediscover a spark I thought might have dimmed, and years of long hours, of prioritizing work and family, had taken their toll. But beneath the surface, the embers of our passion still glow.

"You look stunning tonight," he murmurs, his gaze lingering on me. "That dress..."

"No underwear," I tease, a playful challenge in my voice.

"Really?" he asks, a slow smile spreading across his face.

"You can find out," I retort, a thrill coursing through me.

"I know you would not lie to me," Jamie says as he walks over to my side of the table. He positions himself so he's blocking anyone else's view of me before kissing me while his hand pulls my sundress up a bit. He slides his hands up, spreads my legs, and his fingers find me. He plays with me and then slides two inside. I gasp from surprise and pleasure. I was not expecting him to do that, but it feels fantastic. He slides them in and out of me a few times. He stops kissing me and stands up straight as he pulls his hand away.

"You weren't teasing, but like you said, I needed to find out myself," he says with a wink. "I will be right back. I need to adjust myself in the men's room." Jamie walks away. When he comes back to the table and sits across from me, he leans over as if he's going to tell me a secret.

"I paid the bill. We're going to finish these drinks. Then we're going to go back to the hotel, and I'm going to fuck you so hard and deep. I may lock you in the hotel the rest of the weekend and make you orgasm over and over until you can't walk straight," Jamie tells me.

"Oh," I say, and try to catch my breath. I down the rest of my drink. "Let's go," I command Jamie. He laughs and finishes his drink.

Waking up the next morning, Jamie is not there. I lay there basking in the memory of last night. On our walk back to the hotel, Jamie had asked me to share a sexual fantasy with him. I told him a fantasy of meeting as strangers at a hotel lobby bar, flirting, and getting to know each other over drinks. *We decide to go up to one of our hotel rooms, where we spend the rest of the night having feral sex all over the hotel room.* When we'd gotten back to the hotel, he'd played out my fantasy with me. I can't imagine a better life than the one I have with Jamie. I feel like the luckiest woman in the world. He still takes my breath away every time he walks into a room, and he has only gotten more handsome as we've aged. I notice how still, after all these years, other women look at him when we're out, but he seems oblivious to it. He always ensures I know I'm all he sees, even if he notices.

I hear the hotel door beep as it unlocks. Jamie walks in, balancing a cup of coffee, a fountain soda— Diet Coke, his morning caffeine—and a bag.

"Good morning, beautiful." He smiles at me, his eyes shining brighter than I remember. "I got you a black coffee, no sugar, just as you like it, and croissants for us." I smile at him, appreciating his thoughtfulness. Reaching for my coffee, I sit up and take a sip.

"What is on the agenda for the day?" I ask Jamie as I continue enjoying my coffee.

"Well, first, I am returning to bed with you and enjoying you a bit more. Then we are going to see Bonaventure Cemetery, and then to Broughton Street, which I am told is like our Newbury or Boylston Street. Then we will come back here, have more sex, and clean up. Enjoy happy hour in the lobby. We have a 7:30 dinner reservation at The Pink House. How does that sound?"

"It sounds both exhausting and amazing," I tell him as I look at him over the rim of my coffee cup, taking another sip. Jamie sets his drink down on the nightstand and removes his pants. I notice he's not wearing underwear, and I smile at him. He takes off his shirt, revealing a muscular abdomen with an entire six-pack and defined hip muscle lines right to his erect penis. He crawls across the bed to me, takes the coffee from my hand, and places it on the nightstand behind me as his lips meet mine.

"First on the agenda, I am going to enjoy you a bit more," Jamie whispers in my ear as he wraps his arm around my torso to scoot me down the bed. He lowers me on my back.

"I will be enjoying you just as much as you are enjoying me," I say, looking him in the eyes while I spread my legs and close my eyes as he moves down my body. I am the luckiest woman in the world.

Roaring '20's

Charly & Jamie 2024

We don't get trick-or-treaters like we used to at our house anymore. I buy a small amount of candy, but we usually eat it. Jamie would take JJ and Cari trick-or-treating while I stayed home to pass out candy. I love passing it out to neighborhood kids. Halloween is not the same as when I was growing up, and now that the kids are grown, it is entirely different. Cari is at school in South Carolina, and I'm sure she's in Five Points trying to get into a bar. Just thinking about it makes me anxious.

Back in 1991, when I was at the University of South Carolina-Aiken, I heard stories about Five Points, the bar district in Columbia, SC, where students from the main campus would often go to party. I can't help but think Cari has a fake ID. I'm not naive about what a 19-year-old away at college might do. I've reminded her to please be safe: always buddy up with friends, never accept a drink from someone she doesn't know, and be aware of her surroundings. Jamie has been much more stern with her—he told her to act like a nun, which makes both Cari and me roll our eyes. I want her to have fun but also know how to stay safe.

As for JJ, I hope he's out somewhere in South Boston, where he lives, having a good time. I was hoping that JJ, living with friends, would take some time to relax. He's finishing law school at Suffolk and is very serious about his studies. He's young, and this is the time in his life to have some fun.

Jamie and I decided to have a movie night for Halloween. While Jamie is in the shower, I pop a big bowl of popcorn, open a bottle of wine, and get "Monsters: The Lyle and Eric Menendez Story" ready on Netflix. We invested in the most comfortable couch possible. I love a sectional, and this one has chaise loungers on both ends, making it feel like you're lying on clouds. I enjoy relaxing and ending our days cuddling together on it.

When Jamie joins me on the couch, we start watching the mini-series and talk about our memories of when the events took place. I notice that Jamie is picking up his phone and messaging more than usual, but I don't say anything because I know he has many work demands.

I curl up in Jamie's lap, hoping to distract him from checking his phone. Lying with my head on his lap, Jamie puts his hand under my sweatshirt and begins caressing my breast. I look up at him, smiling. He knows how much I love it when he does that. I can feel him getting hard under me. I sit up and look at him.

"Pause the TV," I say. As he does, I take off my shirt. Jamie leans into me and begins sucking my breast. I moan as he lightly bites my nipples. I push him back as much as I don't want him to stop.

"Take off your pants," I say. I get on my knees on the floor and take his cock into my mouth. Jamie rolls his head back, takes a deep breath, and looks down at me as I look up at him. It turns me on to see how I can please him as much as he pleases me. I suck him, moving my mouth up and down his cock. His breaths become faster. I thought he was going to orgasm. Instead, he stops me, pulls me up, and moves me face down on the couch. He gets behind me, his hand rubbing between my legs to ensure I am wet. He thrusts his cock into me. I let out a little scream. He is rougher than usual, but I like it. He grabs my hair and thrusts hard and fast into me.

"You like that?" he asks me.

"Yes, fuck me harder, faster," I say. It must turn him on because he thrusts harder and faster than ever. "I yell, but he does not stop. He keeps going and thrusting, almost pounding me. He pulls out of me and turns me around to face him. He takes my legs up around his shoulders as he slides back into me. He lifts my hips with one arm, causing me to arch my back. He runs his hands up and down my leg.

"Your legs still drive me crazy after all these years." He leans down and sucks my breast while sliding in and out of me. I wrap my arms around him as I moan in his ear. His body is all muscles. He joined a CrossFit gym a few years ago. It has paid off for him. His body is more muscular than when we first met in our 20s. Sometimes, I cannot believe this handsome, sexy man is all mine. I get to enjoy him and his body whenever I want. After all these years, I still find Jamie to be the most attractive man my eyes can see.

"Jamie, you feel so good inside me, don't stop...I love you so much. You make me feel incredible." Jamie thrusts harder. He then reaches down and begins rubbing my clitoris. His thrusts and rubbing send me into an orgasmic explosion. I scream out, my body trembling. Jamie does not stop. He looks down at me and smiles.

"My turn," he says.

Looking up at him, I say, "Fill me up."

"Oh, I am going to," he replies, moving in and out of me. He speeds up again and brings my legs up and together. I love to be the source of his pleasure. Jamie groans in orgasm.

We lay there in the aftermath of our passion. The great thing about the kids being gone is that we can have impromptu sex whenever and wherever we want; it's like being back before kids.

"That was amazing," I say to Jamie through heavy breaths. As I get up from the couch, Jamie grabs me.

"I want more of you," he says, pulling me back down on the couch. He kisses me and plays with my breast with one hand, and his other hand reaches in between my legs.

"Wow, what's gotten into you tonight?" I say to him as he continues to explore my body. He pulls back and looks at me searchingly in my eyes.

"I love my wife, and I love pleasing her whenever I can," he says, returning to sucking my breast. He begins to rub me harder and faster as I moan and whisper his name. I reach down and feel him hard again. I kiss him and start stroking him. He stops touching me and turns me around. Lying on our sides, spooning, he lifts my top leg and slides into me.

After we both orgasm for the second time, I get up, put my clothes back on, and go to the bathroom to freshen up. At 51, I do not think we will be lucky enough to get a third round. Those days are behind us. I decide to take a quick shower. Jamie comes into the bathroom.

"Remember when we would have sex day and night? We would rush home to have it. We would see how many times in a weekend we could have it and try to beat the weekend before," Jamie reminds me.

"Yes, in our younger days, before we had to start sneaking around not to get caught by the kids," I laugh as I step out of the shower. I look at him in the vanity mirror as I wrap a towel around me.

"The kids are not here anymore. We can do this all the time again. And you don't have to cover yourself," Jamie says, trying to grab the towel from me, but I hold on.

"I am cold and wet. I need it," I say, looking at him. Did he take a Viagra or something? He is horny tonight. He lets me have the towel as he comes behind me and wraps his arms around me.

"I will keep you warm," he whispers as he kisses my neck. He pushes me toward the vanity and starts caressing my breasts as he kisses me.

"Do you really think you can go again?" I ask him. "Because you know how much it turns me on to be fucked over the sink in the bathroom." It's one of the places we would sneak in a quickie when the kids were at home.

"I do," he replies between kisses. He then does something I am not expecting. He turns me around, lifts me onto the sink counter, and goes down on me. I run my fingers through his hair as he does his magic. He looks up at me and says, "Yeah, I am not going to be able to go again, but I am still going to be able to enjoy you."

We finally came up for air and decided to get into bed to spend the rest of the night watching TV together. After a while, I return to the living room to clean up and shut the house down for the night. While there, I grab both phones and notice a notification on Jamie's. It is from his social media account, and I feel anxious when I see it. Something compels me to look closer. I glance down the hall and see him still in bed watching TV. I open his phone and go to the social media account that the notification came from. He has private messages from women, about five in total. Feeling mixed emotions, I slip into the kids' shared bathroom in the hall, lock the door, and begin reading the messages.

After reading two different threads, I feel nauseous and vomit in the toilet. I sit on the floor, trying to process what I've just read. Jamie has been messaging various women, and there are pictures. He talks to them about sex—sex they were having or wanted to have. One of the women is someone he dated in high school until we met. It doesn't seem as though they had had sex. But there is a lot of talk of having feelings for each other. Wishing they could have sex, the different messages were outright sexting.

I quickly begin taking screenshots of the messages and sending them to Kristy and myself. I messaged Kristy, telling her I would explain later and to save the screenshots for me. I am shaking, barely able to see through my tears. I hear Jamie calling for me.

"I'm in the kids' bathroom, my stomach isn't well," I yell, hoping to buy myself some more time. I don't even read the rest of the messages; I screenshot and send them.

"Charly, are you okay?" Jamie asks through the door. I get up off the floor and open the door. There he is, the man I love and had put my faith, trust, and life into.

"Charly, what is wrong? What happened?" Jamie looks at me, frightened. I must look as awful as I feel, which I know I do—my body physically hurts. I hold up his phone for him to see. He glances at the phone and then back at me.

"Did someone call? Did something happen?" he asks, not concerned that I would look at his messages. It seems he thought I was oblivious.

"I need you to pack some things and get the fuck out of this house," I say as calmly as I can.

"What are you talking about?" Jamie responds.

"I need you to pack some things and get the fuck out of this house," I repeat slowly.

"I am not going anywhere," Jamie barks back at me.

"I saw your messages to those women. Is that why you were so horny earlier? Is this why you fucked me so hard tonight? Were you living out a fantasy? Were you thinking of them while you fucked me? Were you using me to practice for them?" Engulfed in tears, I try to catch my breath.

"Charly, no, I am so sorry, shit, I did not want you ever to see those messages," he says.

"Clearly. How many of these women have you slept with?" My voice is getting louder.

"Charly, I will stop, delete the messages, and let you see my phone whenever you want. I will fix this," he pleads to me.

"How many of them have you had sex with?" I yell. Jamie stares at me. I can see it in him. He doesn't want to tell me. I scream again, "*Tell me!*"

Jamie flinches.

"A few," he whispers.

"How many?" I ask again.

"A few, but I love you. I was stupid. Tonight, I made love to you multiple times because I love and desire only you. I realized that and planned to never speak to another woman again. I look at you, and I know I am so lucky, and I feel foolish for even considering doing anything else. I was even more foolish to act on those thoughts."

I can't stand the sight of him. My phone rings on the counter. Looking at it, I see it's Kristy. I reach out to pick it up despite Jamie telling me not to.

"Are you okay?" Kristy questions.

"No," I insist.

"Do you want me to come over or pick you up?" Kristy offers.

"I'm not going anywhere," I say, looking Jamie in the eye as he watches me. "He is getting the hell out of the house," I ask Kristy if she can come over, and I hang up. Jamie continues to stand there, watching me.

"Kristy is on her way over," I say as I walk past him. He grabs my arm to stop me. I turn and look him in the eye.

"Do not touch me, don't you ever touch me again." I can barely walk. I start dry heaving again, turn back to the bathroom, and vomit. Jamie comes up behind me, holds my hair, and rubs my back.

"Get away from me," I scream. Jamie flinches, backs out of the bathroom, and stands in the hall watching me. I lay on the floor, my breath short, my chest feeling tight, and I fear I'm having a heart attack. Tears streak down my cheeks, pooling on the floor.

"Please, Charly, I can't see you like this," Jamie pleads. I ignore him.

I don't know how long I'm on the floor when Kristy comes in. She helps me up and into bed, bringing my favorite drink—an espresso martini. Kristy is a bartender, and I savor her espresso martini.

"I figured you would need one," she says, handing it to me. I sit up in bed, sipping the delicious drink that runs through my body.

"What happened?" Kristy asks. "Never mind, if you don't want to talk about it, you don't have to."

"Those messages I sent you. Jamie has been sleeping with some of the women. I don't know for how long, when, or where. It better have never been in this bed." I look around the room, searching for signs of Jamie with another woman. Suddenly, I realize I don't know if he's left. "Is he still here?" I ask Kristy. She nods.

"Yes, he let me in. He's in the TV room. He said he didn't want to leave you here alone."

"Well, isn't that noble of him to think of me now? Asshole," I say, taking another sip of the martini. I pick up my phone and text Jamie: "LEAVE," then set my phone down. Kristy tells me she'll stay the night with me. I ask her to stay in the room with me, and we find "Golden Girls" on TV.

I wake up to my phone vibrating. It's 4:30 a.m., and I've only been asleep for an hour and a half. There are ten unread text messages from Jamie, but I can't read them now. Nothing he says will change his actions. I glance over at Kristy, still sleeping, and quietly get up to make coffee in the kitchen.

A few hours later, Kristy finds me in the TV room, where I'm playing '80s music on Pandora, staring at nothing. "There's coffee if you want some," I tell her. She goes to the kitchen, grabs a cup, and joins me on the couch.

"What do you want to do?" Kristy asks.

"I know what I need to do, but part of me also doesn't want to do anything," I reply. "We'll need to FaceTime Cari and ask JJ to come home. After that, I guess we'll need to get lawyers involved."

"Are you sure that's what you want? Getting lawyers, I mean. I support you in whatever you decide, but I don't want you to regret anything," Kristy says carefully.

Looking at Kristy and reflecting on her words, my intuition is telling me to leave this relationship. He got caught and admitted to multiple women. Trusting him again seems impossible. I think about young me, the girl I was before Jamie and I were together. I was stronger; I had allowed Jamie to weaken me. I had to ask him to be involved in our finances, essentially. I had to ask him if I could go back to school and go back to work. The Charly before Jamie would not have done that. God, what did I do to myself? What kind of role model have I been to the kids? I want that strength I used to have back.

"I'm sure," I say out loud to Kristy.

Kristy goes home and promises to return with some food for me. She knows I probably won't eat, not because I'm unable to, but because I won't bother to cook anything. Kristy says she will prepare some dishes for me. Although Kristy isn't Italian, she married into an Italian family and, by osmosis, became a fantastic cook, mastering Italian dishes.

I pick up my phone and see several messages from Jamie, but I still can't read them. Instead, I send a message to everyone in the family group chat that we need to have a family meeting. I ask JJ if he can come home tonight, and Cari if she is available to FaceTime tonight. I don't allow Jamie to respond to his availability; he will be there.

Immediately, I received a text from Jamie on our separate chain: "What are you doing?"

I reply, saying we will tell the kids together and that he needs to be at the house when the kids are available. Jamie responds, "I think we need to talk before we talk to the kids."

I tell him I disagree and that this resulted from his actions. My text does not stop him from walking into the house about thirty minutes later. I find him standing in the kitchen. Glaring at him in front of me, he looks smaller to me; his shoulders are slumped, his eyes are pacing over me, and tears are rimming them. Is he going to cry?

"Why?" I ask, with as much calm in my voice as I can muster.

"I don't know, it was a mistake."

"One is a mistake, but this, this is, this is.... something else, ...it's cruel."

"I don't know...you were so busy with the kids for so long, I thought when the kids got older, it would get back to you and me again. Then, you went back to school, you were busy with that, and then you started working. It never became about just you and me again. I felt like you were..."

I wish he had just slapped me across the face, because that might not have hurt as badly as his words did. Fury, that felt like a flame of fire, rises from my toes, into my chest. My legs weaken; I think my head is going to explode.

"I am sorry," Jamie pleads as he steps towards me. I hold up my hands, stopping him, stepping back to form more distance between us.

"Do not come near me. You are fucking.....are you fucking kidding me right now? I was too busy raising our kids, ours, Jamie, *ours!* So that you could go fucking build your dream, you could feel better about being a provider for our children. I gave up my dreams of a career to be the wife you wanted. This person I have become over the last twenty-three years was not who I thought I would be when we first met." I feel as though I am going to lose my mind. "What the fuck...you are standing here telling me that you have been out there fucking other women, is my fault?"

"No, no, that is not what I meant." Shaking his head, flopped defeatedly into a kitchen chair, hanging his head into his hands.

"Look at me," I demand. He looks up at me. "What I just heard you say is, you, you,.....I did not hear any I's in your excuse. Listen, you ...*you* are...a disgusting piece of shit. *Because your wife was home, taking care of your children, not giving you enough attention.* I mockingly say, "You had to go get it somewhere else. Pathetic, you fucking pathetic piece of shit."

I grip the back of a kitchen chair to steady myself. I can't get weak, so he thinks he can or needs to come to my aid. That is what he has been doing all this time. He has been taking care of me, thinking he is rescuing me. I allowed him to. Because that is what I thought being a good wife did. Ugh, it is so antiquated, and not how I wanted to be. How did I let myself be this person?

"Charly, come on, that's not what I meant. I guess I should have said I felt like we grew apart."

"Shut up, shut up, shut up. I heard what you said. You disgust me, I can't stand to look at you, and I don't want to hear a word you are saying. There is no going back from what you have done and said. You can go fuck yourself." I walk out of the kitchen into the bedroom, slamming the door as hard as I can. I crawled back into bed, surrendered to my tears, and fell asleep.

That evening, both kids are available. JJ arrives at the house around 6:30 pm and is thrilled to find Kristy's homemade dishes, immediately heating a piece of lasagna.

"Mom, you don't look good. Are you sick? What's going on? What is with the family meeting? JJ asks, taking a bite.

"Let's wait until your father gets here, and Cari is on FaceTime to discuss things. And thanks for letting me know I look like crap. I have had a rough night." I sit at the dining table watching him eat.

"Mom, if someone died, just tell me, then you can tell Cari." He expresses concern.

"We need to wait." I softly sigh, getting up, realizing I need an alcoholic drink for this.

Jamie arrives around 7 pm, and we FaceTimed Cari. I start the conversation by telling the kids that I had found messages on their father's social media accounts proving he had not just one but a few, as he termed them, "extramarital affairs." Because of this, I tell them I am asking him for a divorce. I look directly into Jamie's eyes as I say that, and he appears shocked. I add that I am sure their father can explain his side of the situation.

Cari begins to cry, and I do my best to comfort her through FaceTime, reassuring her that she will be home in a few weeks and we can be together. JJ remains quiet. I ask him if he wants to talk, but he declines, stating that he needs time to process everything. He then turns to Jamie and says, "Fuck you," before walking back to his bedroom.

Jamie speaks to Cari without me while I sit at the kitchen table with a glass of wine.

"Did that make you feel better?" Jamie glares at me once he returns, sitting across from me.

Looking at him as if he were crazy, I say, "Did sticking your dick in other women make *you* feel better?"

Jamie gets up and starts walking toward the door. He stops, turns to me, and says, "I love you. You are my everything. I messed everything up. I know." I don't know if he is expecting me to say something, but I don't say anything. I stare at him for what feels like ten minutes.

"You can have the house; you can have whatever you want. I just want you to forgive me," He pleads.

"Thanks for the house, but I think it would be best to sell it," I state as emotionless as I can muster.

Jamie walks out. I have no idea where he is going. A part of me wants to know, but another part of me knows I should not care. My life, as I've known it, is gone. It's only been 24 hours, and my life will never be what it was. I feel JJ wrap his arms around me. At times, he reminds me so much of myself, but right now, he reminds me of his father.

Charly 2024

*S*avannah, once a city of strangers, has become my home. Of course, I miss Massachusetts. Thankfully, there are direct flights daily to Boston. I often visit, and my friends and family come to see me frequently. Having found my footing here. I have built a fulfilling career and surrounded myself with a loving community. I've purchased a small bungalow, a cozy haven with a spacious yard perfect for entertaining. I feel I have grown into a woman over the last eight years. I don't know if it is the relaxed way of the southern people or the aesthetics here, but I feel at peace within myself. It is a tangible symbol of my resilience, a testament to the strength I have discovered within myself. The grief, though ever-present, no longer defines me. I have learned to live with it, to honor the memory of our shared life, while embracing the beauty and joy that life still has to offer.

On a hot late summer night, the air carries the scent of jasmine as I watch Prince, my mischievous chihuahua mix, running across the lawn. I adopted him eight months ago from a program out of the Chatham County Sheriff's Office, where I work. As I gaze at the stars twinkling above, I think about my journey to this point in life. The risks I took, the experiences I have had. I wonder what my life would have been like if I had married, especially before I had the opportunity to go to Spain. That was a turning point for me, the moment I realized

I could forge my own path, one that was separate from what was expected of me. In my twenties, I was so desperate for a guy to want me, to choose me, that I didn't even know what I wanted for myself in a relationship. It's a powerful lesson to learn that it's not about being chosen. But it's about understanding what your standards are and choosing someone who aligns with you. At this time in my life, the idea of sharing it with someone special sounds nice. However, I wouldn't be disappointed if he doesn't come along. I no longer feel the need to receive a man's love to feel worthy. I realize my friendships are what have kept me going all these years. From meeting Marie in third grade, my other Danvers Girls, Melissa, my friends in Boston, Tonya, and now Celeste. With each experience or job I have had, I have gained lifelong friends. I recently read a quote on social media. I don't know who said it, but it read **"I think we subconsciously undervalue platonic love and intimacy from our friends because society puts so much emphasis on finding and having romantic love. I don't know about you, but I wouldn't be shit without the unending love and support of my friends."** *Those words explained my life to me. My friends have been the external love that has helped me feel secure in myself, allowing me to be vulnerable and loved. In the end, my friends have been and will be my life's greatest loves.*

Wednesday mornings are always tough to start once I arrive at the office after my weekly 7:30 a.m. community meeting. The meeting still reverberates in my head, a cacophony of voices. Sitting at my desk, staring at the computer, unanswered emails loom. The thought of tackling the day's agenda fills me with a sense of dread, a

longing for anything but mundane. And so, I succumb to the siren call of distraction. With a sigh, I open the LinkedIn app on my phone. I always feel as though I am still "working." If I am on LinkedIn, I may find an article on how to be an effective manager. Perhaps, I think, a glimpse into the professional lives of others, their passions, and their triumphs might ignite a spark within me, a flicker of inspiration to face the day with renewed vigor.

I see a notification that someone wants to connect. Intrigued, I click, my brow furrowing slightly. "James Walsh?" The name sparks a flicker of recognition. I hurry to my laptop, eager to investigate further. And then it hits me. My hands tremble, the keyboard suddenly feeling foreign beneath my fingertips. Jamie. Jamie Walsh.

It's been at least a decade, maybe even more, since his name has crossed my mind. Not that I've forgotten him entirely. His ghost occasionally haunts my memories, most notably in the form of a well-worn anecdote. A jolt of excitement, a thrilling flutter of anticipation, courses through me. What did he want? The possibilities, both exhilarating and terrifying, dance before my eyes.

My heart leaps as I see his message, the words blurring slightly. I barely read them as I begin to type a message back. "Hey stranger," I type, the phrase echoing through the years. How incredible to hear from him after all this time. His profile picture, a window into the present, takes my breath away. He is even more handsome now, the years seemingly having only deepened his appeal. He responds quickly.

Jamie: Hi, you came up as someone I may know. Seeing your name brought a smile to my face. How are you?

Me: I am good. I'm living in Savannah, Georgia. I am glad you reached out. I would hate for you to have seen my profile and not message me for months. To only run into each other at a concert next summer. LOL

Jamie: Ha Ha, we were so silly not to talk to each other then. But once we did, there was no separating us.

Me: I know, we were attached at the hip. Why did we stop being friends? I liked you so much, more than friends.

Jamie: I don't know, I know it was you're doing and I was sad about it. I had no idea you liked me more than a friend. I was really into you.

Me: Hmmm, I don't remember.

Jamie: So, tell me all about what you have been up to? I want to hear all your successes. I remember you being so intelligent. I imagined you would go far in life.

As we exchange messages, sharing snippets of our lives, a wave of nostalgia washes over me. The memory of our chance encounter at Square One Mall resurfaces as a poignant reminder of our history. Yet, it's tinged with a bittersweet ache. He had seemed aloof that day, almost irritated by my presence. I'd been convinced I'd somehow annoyed him, that my presence was a burden, a constant irritant during our college years. The image of him practically fleeing the scene still lingers, a painful reminder of my misunderstanding of how he felt for me.

And now, here he is, his messages brimming with warmth and genuine delight that surprised me. He is genuinely interested in my life and eager to hear about my successes. As we reminisce about our friendship, the years seem to melt away.

Jamie: I remember you asking me to be your A&P lab partner. I was psyched. LOL

Me: I did! I don't remember asking you. Do you remember how freaked out I got in the lab when we had to skin the cat? OMG, so to this day, I eat people's French fries, and I tell people the story of how you started buying two orders of French fries.

Jamie: I loved that you ate my fries. It made me feel good that you were that comfortable with me. I was happy to buy two orders to see you eat them.

He continues to fill in the gaps, painting vivid pictures of shared experiences and intimate and profound moments, awakening a flood of long-forgotten emotions: a bittersweet longing, a wistful yearning for what might have been, stirred within me. He is undoubtedly happy in his life. He's lived a whole life of a successful career, marriage, and family.

Me: I honestly thought you thought of me as a silly girl, just floating around laughing.

Jamie: Not at all. I wanted a lot more than friendship with you. But, as I said, you made it very clear that you did not want anything more from me.

Lost in the haze of time, I am surprised by his confession, admitting to a longing he'd kept hidden, a desire for a love that transcended the boundaries of friendship. But fate, it seemed, had had other plans. He'd believed my sudden withdrawal was a consequence of my involvement with Peter Finley. I shared that it was untrue that Peter and I had not gotten together until after graduation, two years after Jamie and I had stopped talking. Now, with the wisdom and confidence of adulthood, we finally lay bare our unspoken feelings, the echoes of a love that might have been.

Over days of exchanging messages, our conversation takes a more intimate turn, revisiting the night we had shared at his mother's apartment, the raw passion and unspoken longing that had filled the air. He reminisces about other nights out at bars or times alone, the countless teases and playful banter, the unspoken promise of something more. A memory of a song comes up for me.

Me: Are you the one I had asked about a Nine Inch Nails song?

Jamie: Yes, "Closer," you loved that song. You were so funny telling me about it. You put the CD on one night when I was in your bedroom.

The memory of that night, the intensity of our connection, fills me with both embarrassment and a yearning for what might have been.

Me: Oh, poor young Charly, with her naive hopes and dreams, had tried so hard with you.

Jamie's memories of me remain vivid and poignant, a testament to the intensity of our connection that had been unknown to me. We also reminisce about our simpler moments, the countless hours spent sitting together on campus, laughing and sharing about our lives. The image of us sharing lunch, his tall frame protectively shielding me from the world, brings a warm smile to my face. Those were the moments that defined our friendship, the unspoken bond. Jamie and I had spent a year building a connection in our bubble on the peninsula of the UMass Boston campus. A year no one knew about. Now, here we could validate that it was real, it happened, and our feelings were mutual.

"So, you have no memory as to why you two stopped being friends?" Melissa asks. I had just finished telling her and Celest about the resurfacing of Jamie. Melissa has started joining Celeste and me for our weekly date.

"Also, I can't believe you had this whole situationship with this guy, and I had no idea." Melissa takes a sip of wine.

"First off, we didn't call it a situationship back then, and you and I were newly friends. I most likely would not have said anything. But yeah, I cannot remember why we stopped being friends." I gulp down the rest of my wine.

"Do you think he was bad in bed?" Celeste makes a face by clenching her teeth and sucking in air.

"I don't remember what it was like," I admit, looking up as if maybe the answer is on the ceiling.

Over the next few days, as I reflect on my life with Jamie, it has stirred up a range of emotions in me. I try so hard to recall why we'd stopped communicating; it feels as if we faded away from each other. It is Halloween, the sun is shining, and the weather is warm. The kids here in the south have no idea how lucky they are to have warm Halloweens. Growing up in Massachusetts, you're likely to need a jacket over your costume. As I drive home from the office, I open the car sunroof and turn on '90s alternative music. I see train gates go down and traffic slow down. I put my car in park, settle back into my seat to feel the sun on my face. Then it hits me. The memory comes rushing back: the condom filled with sausages! I can see it, and remembering Jamie was on his way to my house, I fell asleep. But wait.... it wasn't him. Michelle and Jen N. had told me years ago that it was them. Tears start filling my eyes. For fuck's sake, slamming my hands on the steering wheel. By the time I get home, I am filled with emotion. I lost a fantastic guy. I log on to my computer and send a message to Jamie.

Me: I remember why I stopped talking to you. I had fallen asleep the night you were supposed to come over. When I left to go to work the next morning, I found a condom stuffed with breakfast sausages on my parents' front steps. I assumed you'd left it there. It felt like you were showing that you thought of me as just a hook-up. But back in 2010, at a holiday party, two of my friends told me they were the ones who'd left it.

Instantly, Jamie messages: I would never do something like that, even back then.

Me: I know now! Well, and when they told me it was them.

As I lay in bed that night, all I could think of was why I didn't ask him about it then. Why didn't I think more about things, like how he would have had sausages in his car? There were no late-

night stores back then for him to run to. Instead, I chose to stop talking to him altogether. Now, I couldn't help but laugh at myself. I wish I could go back and tell young Charly to speak up. She was so hesitant, so afraid of rejection. She wanted to be chosen so badly that she didn't want to scare a guy away by questioning him. I think about Jamie sharing that after we stopped talking, he returned to his high school girlfriend and married her. I told him what Jessica had told me, and he assured me there was no overlap between us. He is still happily married to her twenty-six years later. They have two children in their twenties who appear to be the world to him. The same wife and job for all these years, talk about a man who commits.

Jamie and I continue exchanging messages in the following weeks, sharing more highlights from our lives over the past thirty-one years. One Sunday morning, I woke up overwhelmed with emotion. I can't stop crying and want to express my feelings to Jamie.

Me: Jamie, your popping back into my life has brought up a lot of emotions and memories. I remember liking you a lot. I remember I liked being around you. I felt taken care of and protected when I was with you. You made my face light up. I didn't think you felt the same way toward me. I didn't know you took me seriously, and I felt like I was just a hook-up for you. I was afraid to tell you how I felt because I feared rejection. And I'm sure at the time I thought I would rather be your friend than be nothing, so for you to tell me that you did have feelings for me, I'm sad that we stopped being around each other. It brings up regret in me—something I don't like to have. I have a memory of one day going into the lab. We must've had a holiday break. We hadn't seen each other for a bit. You were already at the table. You turned on the stool as I sat down. You looked at me, put your hands on my legs, and said, "I missed you." At that moment, my heart exploded. Maybe this was when he'd realize he wanted to be more than friends with me, I thought. He will ask me on a date.

This is all to say, it's super hard to hear that it was the opposite of what I thought. But it was also lovely to hear that there were feelings for me. I wasn't just imagining our connection.

Everything happens for a reason. We went on the journeys in life that we were meant to go on. It is nice to put closure to a what-if in my life. I am so happy for you and the family and the life you've built. I am so proud to see what a fantastic man you turned out to be. Thank you for being a wonderful memory and chapter in my life.

Thank you for popping back in. It has been helpful for me to reflect on and learn lessons for my ongoing self-growth.

Jamie once again quickly writes back.

Charly, I adored you and was very hurt when you stopped talking to me. And it was clear it was on your terms.

Tears stream down my face as I reread Jamie's message. With a pang of bittersweet longing, I wonder how my life would have unfolded had I not stumbled upon that stupid prank. Would I have been the woman standing beside him at the altar four years later? The thought was both exhilarating and devastating. My life, a carefully constructed tapestry of experiences, would have been irrevocably altered. The friends I cherish, the adventures I'd embarked upon—Spain, the vibrant pulse of Boston, my own "Sex and the City" escapade—none of that would have existed.

Despite the happiness I've cultivated, a nagging doubt creeps in. Had I, in my youthful naivete, let the person who could have given me everything I have been looking for go? The man who had unknowingly been the blueprint for every romantic ideal I'd harbored. The realization hits me with the force of a tidal wave, a profound sense of regret washing over me. I've always prided myself on living without regrets, embracing each twist and turn of fate. But now, this unexpected resur-

facing of my past has unearthed a subconscious yearning, a gaping wound. It is hard not to wonder what would have happened if Jamie and I had dated.

Me: If I had told you how I felt back then, would we have ended up dating?

Jamie: 100%, absolutely. Don't you think? I was so scared to tell you how I felt. If you had told me, I would have been thrilled.

Me: I know I would have been all in if you had asked me out.

Jamie: Stupid kids with no communication skills.

Me: Well, I am a firm believer that everything happens for a reason. You were meant to go your way, and I was meant to go mine.

But I still think about it. What if we'd gotten together, married, and had children? Would we still be married? I have lived a life opposite to his. I do wonder what life would be like if I had married a man who loved me and was committed to me the way Jamie is dedicated to his wife and children.

The most surreal thought is how life can change with a single decision. Sitting here, looking out the window and contemplating all this, I vividly remember the morning I stepped onto my parents' porch, gazing down at the steps in horror at what I saw. Who would have guessed that a prank of a condom and some breakfast sausage would change the trajectory of my life?

Charly.........& Jamie 2025

I'm sitting on the bench Jamie had built, the wood still warm from the afternoon sun. The moving truck, a jarring symbol of the end, disap

I'm sitting on the bench Jamie had built, the wood still warm from the afternoon sun. The moving truck, a jarring symbol of the end, disappears down the street, swirling dust and fallen leaves in its wake. This is the last time I'll sit on this bench in front of this house, the last time I'll gaze at this familiar neighborhood. Memories flood back: Cari's colorful chalk drawings, JJ and his friends playing street hockey, lemonade stands, and our evening walks. We built a beautiful life here, a life that now feels like a distant dream.

Jamie approaches, his face a mixture of guilt and uncertainty. "Just making sure everything is cleaned up," he says.

I barely acknowledge him; the weight of his betrayal is still heavy in my heart. He sits beside me, and I shift away, the physical distance mirroring the emotional wedge that will always separate us.

"I'm truly sorry, Charly," he says, his voice a mere whisper. But his apologies ring hollow, a futile attempt to once again mend what is broken.

"You did what you did," I say, my voice firm. "Our marriage is over."

The past year has been filled with meetings with lawyers, tears, and the slow, agonizing process of disentangling our lives. My new life awaits me in Boston, a two-bedroom apartment in the North End, a place I've dreamed of living since college—a life I might have had had I not chosen love and commitment over my own ambitions.

"I did everything I could for you, for our family," I say to him. He looks at me, surprised to hear me speak endearingly to him. Lately, our interactions have been reduced to curt exchanges and icy glares from me. Silent, he looks tenderly, and I can see his love for me.

Sitting here, I wonder... what if? What if I had pursued my dreams and embraced the unknown, not believing that a man was what I needed to be successful in life? I had thought that if a man chose me, then I was worthy. I had wanted to be chosen so badly. Who would I have become? The question hangs heavily in the air, a bittersweet echo of what might have been. But I will never know, movies are made about how we met, and how I fell in love with him. The future beckons, a blank canvas to paint a new life. A life filled with new adventures and the promise of healing and self-discovery. I will cherish every moment with JJ and Cari as they embark on their adulthood journeys. I will be civil with Jamie for their sake when we have to be together for them. But this journey with Jamie has closed. Boston, a city with vibrant energy, awaits me to begin living the life I always imagined when I was in college.

Standing at the car door, I take one last look at the house. Jamie sits on the bench, a solitary figure against the backdrop of a life that once was. Memories of the children, their laughter, echo through the air. A bittersweet ache washes over me.

I take a deep breath as I back out of the driveway and the house shrinks in the rearview mirror. I decide to stop to get a roast beef downtown for one last time. I can't get them in the city.

With each mile that separates me from the house, a sense of closure settles over me. It's a quiet acknowledgment of acceptance. The past, with all its joys and sorrows, has found its place. Now, a new chapter awaits, a journey filled with possibilities. This North Shore girl is finally making it over the Tobin Bridge.

Get ready to discover your new favorite author!
Charity C. Collier bursts onto the literary scene with her debut novel, "Making It Over The Tobin Bridge"!

A true New Englander at heart, Charity's roots run deep in the North Shore of Boston, Massachusetts. She didn't just visit Boston; she *lived* it, spending most of her adult life in the vibrant heart of the city, where she lived, worked, and soaked in its unique energy. It's this firsthand experience that infuses her writing with authenticity. She finds immense joy in crafting stories that navigate the tapestry of life in Boston and the North Shore with compelling narratives of love, what-ifs, and self-discovery.

Charity isn't just an author; she's a storyteller immersed in the real stuff of life, ready to share her unique voice and vibrant world with readers everywhere!

I want to extend my sincere gratitude to many people. There are so many friends I wanted to put in this book. When I received the first edit, I was told I had too many people in it. I laughed, because I have that many and more. Every person who has touched my life has helped me write this and my future books.

I'm so proud to be from Danvers, MA, and it was a joy to use my North Shore and Boston roots as the backdrop for this story. Thank you, Tayler Simon, for giving me the courage to do this. If I had not met you, I don't think I would have done it. Thank you, Mary Bassett, for being my first reader of the first draft and for believing in the story. While your character may not have made it into the final version, your support was invaluable.

It was hard to write about Tina (the real Marie). Tina was also the inspiration for Charly Walsh as a mother. The pain I felt while writing about Tina's passing in May 2022 was so profound that I ultimately decided to keep her character alive in the story. Similarly, the death of the real Mark changed me, and I hope both Tina and Paul would be proud of how their stories are honored in these pages.

Lastly, love to my Mom, Dad, and Travis. The three of them have been front-row audience members in my life. They have always made me feel loved and accepted.